ODDS AGAINST SURVIVAL

Skye didn't like his chances. There were five hard-bitten men in the locked hotel room, all with guns at the ready. There was one of him, and his gun was gone. Then there was the girl, tied up like a lamb waiting for the slaughter while her captors savored what they were going to do with her and to her.

"We gonna take him with us? one of the men asked the leader, Willie.

"No," said Willie. "But we get rid of him quietly. No noise, no fuss."

"Maybe we just shoot him here, use a pillow," the rat-faced one said.

"That just might do it, Jimmy," Willie said with a smile that was more of a snarl. He looked at Fargo. "Get over there, against that wall."

If Skye wanted to make his move, it had to be now. Trouble was, any move he made landed him straight in the grave. But maybe it was worth finding out how many of these trail dogs he could take with him....

THE
TRAILSMAN
142

GOLDEN
BULLETS

by

Jon Sharpe

A SIGNET BOOK

SIGNET
Published by the Penguin Group
Penguin Books USA Inc., 375 Hudson Street,
New York, New York 10014, U.S.A.
Penguin Books Ltd, 27 Wrights Lane,
London W8 5TZ, England
Penguin Books Australia Ltd, Ringwood,
Victoria, Australia
Penguin Books Canada Ltd, 10 Alcorn Avenue,
Toronto, Ontario, Canada M4V 3B2
Penguin Books (N.Z.) Ltd, 182-190 Wairau Road,
Auckland 10, New Zealand

Penguin Books Ltd, Registered Offices:
Harmondsworth, Middlesex, England

First published by Signet, an imprint of Dutton Signet,
a division of Penguin Books USA Inc.

First Printing, October, 1993
10 9 8 7 6 5 4 3 2 1

The first chapter of this book previously appeared in *Tomahawk Justice*,
the one hundred forty-first volume in this series.

 REGISTERED TRADEMARK—MARCA REGISTRADA

Printed in the United States of America

PUBLISHER'S NOTE
This is a work of fiction. Names, characters, places, and incidents either are
the product of the author's imagination or are used fictitiously, and any
resemblance to actual persons, living or dead, events, or locales is entirely
coincidental.

BOOKS ARE AVAILABLE AT QUANTITY DISCOUNTS WHEN USED TO PROMOTE PROD-
UCTS OR SERVICES. FOR INFORMATION PLEASE WRITE TO PREMIUM MARKETING DIVI-
SION, PENGUIN BOOKS USA INC., 375 HUDSON STREET, NEW YORK, NEW YORK 10014.

The Trailsman

Beginnings ... they bend the tree and they mark the man. Skye Fargo was born when he was eighteen. Terror was his midwife, vengeance his first cry. Killing spawned Skye Fargo, ruthless, cold-blooded murder. Out of the acrid smoke of gunpowder still hanging in the air, he rose, cried out a promise never forgotten.

The Trailsman they began to call him all across the West: searcher, scout, hunter, the man who could see where others only looked, his skills for hire but not his soul, the man who lived each day to the fullest, yet trailed each tomorrow. Skye Fargo, the Trailsman, the seeker who could take the wildness of a land and the wanting of a woman and make them his own.

1860. The Black Hills of South Dakota and the yellow gold of greedy, devious men . . .

1

"I think I'm in the wrong room," Fargo said, and realized the remark was so obvious it was stupid. But it was the first thing that came to his lips.

"You sure as hell are, mister," the heavy-jawed man rasped. The hotel room key still in his hand, Fargo's eyes swept the room again, taking in the five men and, on the settee, the young woman bound hand and foot, a kerchief gagging her mouth. He had time to take in only a round-cheeked face and brown hair pinned atop her head, and in her eyes, a desperate plea for help. But the room was too small for him to draw on the five men. Besides, he hadn't any idea of what the strange scene meant.

"I'll just go on my way," he said.

"The hell you will," the heavy-jawed man said.

"The desk clerk gave me the wrong room key, must be a duplicate," Fargo said, and started to move toward the door. Three of the men rose, guns drawn.

"Get his gun," the big-jawed one said, and Fargo cursed softly as one of the others drew the Colt from his holster. Fargo stayed motionless. It wasn't the time to act.

"What are we gonna do with him, Willie?" one of the others asked, a thin, wiry-bodied man with a rat-like face.

"I'll figure something," the one called Willie said.

Skye Fargo's glance flicked to the young woman where she lay on the settee, her blue skirt raised enough to show nicely curved thighs. In her eyes she managed to add sympathy to the desperate pleading. "Get over there, against that wall," Willie ordered, and Fargo retreated to stand against the far wall of the room. A window was but a foot away, he noted with a surreptitious glance. The room was on the ground floor of the hotel, raised some six feet from the ground. Fargo brought his eyes back to the five men.

"We gonna take him with us?" one of the others asked, a short, thick-set figure with a fleshy face.

"No," Willie snapped. "But we get rid of him quietly, no noise and no fuss."

"Maybe we just shoot him here, use a pillow, and leave him for the maid to find come morning," the rat-faced one said.

"That might just do it, Jimmy," Willie said with a smile that was more of a snarl. He stepped to where the young woman lay bound and gagged. "I'd like to do the same with you, honey, only we got orders about you."

"Maybe we can get to enjoy her afterwards," Jimmy said, his rat-like face folding into anticipation.

"Maybe," Willie agreed, and shot a glance at Fargo. "You watching him?" he barked at the others and they all nodded. Fargo allowed a grim smile inside himself. He had already edged six inches closer to the window, sliding his feet along the floor. The big-jawed man paced the room, plainly nervous. "Damn, I hate waiting as much as I hate unexpected things," he growled, and tossed another glance at Fargo.

"How long we have to wait?" the fleshy-faced one asked.

"Another half-hour," Willie snapped, and resumed his pacing. Fargo had reached the edge of the window frame, his eyes moving over the other four men. They were paying as much attention to Willie's pacing and the young woman as they were to him. Slowly, he half-turned, his back to the window, and drew in a deep breath as he gathered the muscles of his powerful calves and thighs. He counted off three to himself and, tightening his every muscle, catapulted himself backward, arching his body as he crashed into the window. "Jesus," he heard Willie snarl as he went out the window in a shower of glass.

Outside, in mid-air, he twisted his body as he fell and landed on his side on ground that he gratefully found had a soft top cover of loose soil. He rolled, glanced up at the broken window and saw Willie's face, lips drawn back, the gun in his hand. But he didn't fire, Fargo noted. "Go after him. Get him, goddammit, get him," the man shouted, and Fargo heard the sound of running feet as he rose and raced from the side of the hotel. It would only take moments for the men to reach the front of the hotel and come around after him and he ran back, past a series of low-roofed sheds and darkened buildings.

Spying the entrance to a dark alleyway, he dropped to one knee and waited. The three men appeared in moments, racing around the side of the hotel to pause under the window. "He went that way," Willie shouted at them and Fargo rose and ran through the alleyway as the three figures started toward him. The other end of the alleyway opened onto a series of narrow streets and alleys, most between low-roofed sheds. He chose an alley and raced down it. He paused halfway down, listening, and heard the three figures come to a halt, exchange muttered oaths, and break off on their own. He listened a moment longer, heard one moving toward the alley where he waited and he ran on, dodged around the end corner, and flattened himself against the wall of the shed. He heard the footsteps come down the alley, hurrying. The man would have his gun in hand, Fargo knew, and he dropped into a crouch, turned, and waited. The man moved from the alley and tried to pause to glance about, when the diving body hurtled into him from the side.

He went down and his shot went wild. He tried to bring his gun around but Fargo's blow slammed into his jaw and his head snapped sideways. Fargo got one hand around the six-gun, twisted, and pulled it from the man's grasp. He started to draw a bead on the man when he heard the other footsteps racing toward him. He began to rise to his feet to flee but the man jumped up, trying to wrap both arms around him. His chest slammed into the six-gun and Fargo heard it go off, his finger jarred by the blow. The figure slid lifelessly from him to collapse on the ground, and Fargo rolled as the other two raced out of the alley.

Unused to the gun, he fired two shots too quickly and cursed as both missed. He dived and rolled as a flurry of bullets whistled past him. Coming up against the base of a shed, he stayed flattened on the ground, got off another two shots, and saw one of his pursuers clutch at his upper arm. But it was a shot that only grazed and both men ran forward firing. Fargo pulled the trigger and heard the sound of an empty chamber, glanced down at the gun and cursed as he saw it was a five-shot Joslyn army revolver. Discarding the gun to use both hands, he rolled, catapulted himself forward, and heard the shots slam into the shed just over his back. But he had reached the mouth of another alley and he rose and raced forward. No shots followed as they paused to reload and he kept running, darting through the night from one dark passage to another, feeling not unlike a rat in a maze.

He halted finally, listened, and heard no footsteps coming after him. They had broken off the pursuit. He leaned against a shed, drew a deep breath, and began to pull what had happened into place. It was only a few hours ago that he'd finished breaking a new trail into Green Valley for a large herd. After a few bourbons with Ted Towers and a good paycheck in his pocket, he had decided that a good night's rest at a room in a proper hotel was very much in order. He'd ridden into Council Bluffs, left the Ovaro at a well-run stable, and gone to the hotel. The desk clerk had set the rest in motion by giving him a duplicate key to the wrong room. The sight that had greeted him flashed instantly before him.

The thing that burned inside him was the terrible plea in a young woman's light-brown eyes. Going back alone would be to invite death again. He needed help. Council Bluffs was no way-station town with neither law nor order. A major port on the Missouri, growing every year, it had to have a proper sheriff. Fargo made his way through the back alleys to emerge on a cobblestone street bordering the waterfront. He spied an old man sitting atop a cotton bale and halted before him. "I want to find the sheriff," he said.

"Don't expect he'll be at his office at this hour," the man said. "But he lives not far away, down Beacon Street, sixth house from the corner."

"Where's Beacon Street?" Fargo queried.

"Three streets and turn left," the man said. "What you want with the sheriff at this hour?"

"I'm not sure," Fargo said, and the man's face creased into a deep frown. Fargo followed the directions, found Beacon Street, and counted off six houses to halt before a neat, brick building. SHERIFF DUPRY—RESIDENCE, a neat sign said beside the door. Fargo used the brass knocker and in a few moments the door opened. He faced a medium-height man, with a square face and hair beginning to gray, clothed in trousers and an undershirt. "Sorry to bother you," Fargo said. "Name's Fargo, Skye Fargo. Some call me the Trailsman."

"Ted Towers hired you to cut him a new trail from the north," the sheriff said. Apparently Council Bluffs was not too big for news to travel, Fargo noted as he nodded.

"Came into town for a good night's sleep. It hasn't turned out that way yet," Fargo said, and quickly recounted what had happened after he'd reached the hotel.

"We got seven hotels and boarding houses here to accommodate folks from the riverboats. Where was this?" Sheriff Dupry asked.

"Place called Council Inn," Fargo said, "only a few blocks from the waterfront. I'd say that young woman was in trouble and I'd like to find out more."

"Wait here. I'll get my gun," the sheriff said. He disappeared into the house for a moment and returned wearing a shirt with a star fixed to the front and a big Remington in the holster of his gunbelt. He set off at a brisk walk and Fargo found himself stretching his legs to keep up with him.

"Room five," Fargo said when they reached the hotel, and the sheriff strode to the desk.

"What happened in room five tonight, Ed?" he

14

asked brusquely. The desk clerk, a balding, older man, looked fearful.

"Don't rightly know. They busted the window, I know that," the clerk said.

"Who did?" Fargo questioned.

"Somebody. Don't really know that, either."

"Let's have a look," the sheriff said, and Fargo followed him down the corridor. The sheriff knocked, knocked again harder, and stepped back when there was no answer. "Open up. This is the sheriff," he called out. Silence was the only reply. He closed a hand around the doorknob, drew the Remington from its holster, and turned the knob. The door opened, swung wide, and Fargo stared into the room. It was empty, pieces of the shattered window glass still on the floor. The sheriff checked the adjoining washroom. "Nothing in there," he muttered. "Let's go back to old Ed."

He returned to the desk clerk, who still looked fearful. "Who rented that room from you, Ed?" he asked.

"Miss Darby, Bess Darby," the clerk said, and turned his ledger book for the sheriff to see. "She arrived this afternoon."

"Who were the five men?" the sheriff questioned.

"They said they were friends of hers, wanted to surprise her. I gave them the room number," the clerk said.

"Did you see them leave together?" Sheriff Dupry asked.

"Didn't see anybody leave," the clerk said. "Heard the window crash but that's all."

"They left by the window, took the girl out that way," Fargo put in.

"It'd seem so." The sheriff nodded grimly. "You say you got one of them. Let's have a look." Fargo led the way to where the still figure lay on the ground, and the sheriff turned the man onto his back. "Never seen him before," Dupry muttered. "They made off with her, that's for sure."

"And with my Colt. I want them both back," Fargo said.

"Hell, we can't search all of Council Bluffs," Sheriff Dupry said. "Even with my two deputies it'd take a week. The waterfront alone is full of storage sheds and warehouses. I'm sorry, but I don't see a hell of a lot we can do."

"They were holding her. They had orders to take her somewhere. I keep seeing her eyes pleading with me to help her," Fargo said.

"I'm sure that'll haunt you, boy, but we don't have a clue where to begin. A young woman stops in Council Bluffs. That's not unusual. We don't know where she was from or where she was going or why she was here. And we sure as hell don't know why anybody'd be making off with her." Fargo nodded, aware of the truth in the sheriff's words. "It'll be one of those things you'll be wondering about for years to come. They happen."

"I don't like wondering," Fargo said glumly. "But thanks for helping. I appreciate that."

"I'd get that room you were supposed to have and that good night's sleep you came for," the sheriff said.

"I think that's good advice," Fargo said. He exchanged a handshake with the man and took a new room key from the desk clerk.

"I'm sorry about everything," the clerk said apologetically.

"Mistakes happen. This one might have saved a young woman's life," Fargo said, and the clerk shrugged helplessly. The new room was at the end of the corridor and Fargo went in, put the bolt on, and undressed. He stretched out on the sheets, trail weariness sweeping over him. He should have slept like the proverbial log. Instead, he found himself tossing, turning, waking, and each time he woke he saw a pair of pleading eyes. He managed to get in enough sleep in short spurts but he snapped awake with the first light of dawn, quickly washed and dressed, and hurried down the silent corridor to the room of mistakes. He entered and stepped to the window, swung one leg over the sill, and lowered himself to the ground.

He scanned the marks, saw where he had landed and then run. He also saw the footprints of the three men who'd chased after him, all clearly outlined. But that's all he saw, and a furrow dug into his brow as he scanned the ground again. There were no other prints. "Goddamn," he murmured. "They didn't go out the window with her." Cold anger rising inside him, he strode around to the front of the still-silent hotel and into the entrance. The desk clerk was asleep, his balding head lying on the desk, half on the register. He woke when he felt the powerful arm around his neck and hands starting to turn his head.

"What . . . what's this?" he gasped out, most of his wind cut off by Fargo's arm.

"It's very early. Nobody's going to hear your neck snap if you don't level with me, you little bastard," Fargo hissed.

"Oh, God, oh, God," the clerk managed.

Fargo turned the man's head a fraction more and the clerk uttered a strangled sound of pain and panic. "Where did they take her?" Fargo demanded.

"I don't know," the man said.

"But they passed you with her."

"Yes, four of them, one carrying her over his

17

shoulder. They said they'd come back and kill me if I talked," the clerk said.

"I'll kill you now if you don't," Fargo said.

"I just told you all I know."

"Which way did they go with her?" Fargo pressed. "Don't tell me you didn't watch them."

"They carried her off, that's all I know. They went outside with her and kept going."

"No horses?"

"No. They walked off with her, east toward the river," the clerk said, and Fargo uttered a silent groan. She could be at the bottom of the Missouri by now. He released his grip on the clerk's head and neck and the little man let himself lay half across the desk, gasping in gulps of air. But he had told everything he knew, Fargo was certain. He'd been too terrified for further lies. Fargo left him and strode outside in the new morning. He walked the few streets to the riverfront where some of the waterfront activity was already beginning, crates being moved, freight wagons arriving. Fargo's eyes swept the scene. Something was missing but he couldn't decide what. He frowned as he surveyed the waterfront again and suddenly an oath exploded from his lips as he stared at the end of the short dock almost directly in front of him.

It was empty. But a stern-wheel river boat had been there when he'd passed yesterday afternoon. He saw a small shack with a sign reading DOCKMASTER on it and he ran to it. He was jumping to conclusions, he knew, yet it fit. The men had orders to bring her someplace and they hadn't used horses to carry her off. The river boat would have been only a few streets' walk. He pulled the door of the shack open to find a man sipping his morning coffee, still in his undershirt and suspenders, a dockmaster's cap hanging on a wall peg behind him.

"That stern-wheeler that was tied up here last night, where is she?" Fargo barked.

"That'd be the *Missouri Belle*. She sailed on the midnight tide," the dockmaster said.

"Sailed where?" Fargo snapped.

"Upriver."

"What's her next stop?"

"Sioux City," the dockmaster said.

"When is she due there?" Fargo pressed.

"Late afternoon. The Missouri gets real narrow in places between here and Sioux City. She'll be making slow time."

"She stopping there overnight?"

"No, just for three hours; long enough to take on more fuel. She'll be sailing come dark," the man said. "Upriver to Yankton."

"Much obliged," Fargo said as he hurried away. Minutes later, he was at the public stable saddling his well-rested horse. When he rode from Council Bluffs he turned the Ovaro to follow the course of the river and kept a steady, ground-eating pace, using level ground whenever possible but always staying within sight of the Missouri as it snaked its way northward. Perhaps it was all a wild-goose chase, he realized, but he'd see it through. Without a gun, he grunted. He had decided that time was more important than staying to buy one. Besides, he didn't want just any gun. He wanted his Colt back, a finely-honed weapon he knew as well as he did the back of his hand.

Fargo rested the Ovaro twice at small lakes he came upon. The afternoon sun was moving downward toward the horizon when he finally caught sight of the river boat as it paddled its way almost in the center of the Missouri. It's low main deck only a few feet above water, it moved with a stately grace, the tall, thin smokestacks with their fluted tops seeming more decorative than practical. The stern paddle wheel created only a thin white froth of water. The *Missouri Belle* was moving slowly, and he saw why as he spotted the crewman at the bow using a sand-bar pole.

Fargo slowed the Ovaro and kept pace with the river boat as the craft wound its way through the treacherous sections of the river. Sand bars, a captain's nightmare, were constantly shifting, one place one week and another the following week. But he saw the boat begin to edge closer to the shore and in the distance he spied the buildings of Sioux City. He sent the Ovaro forward and reached the town some twenty minutes ahead of the river boat. He threaded his way along the waterfront crowded with roustabouts, saw the main dock, and moved the pinto behind a tall storage shed. He dismounted and moved forward on foot, picking his way through stacks of crates and barrels, boxes and bales, as he saw the *Missouri Belle* nose its way into the dock. He found a spot behind an empty Owensboro platform spring dray that afforded him a good view of the gangplank area and settled down to watch and wait.

A dozen passengers disembarked and a handful boarded. Mostly it was work crews bringing off freight and others starting to carry cords of firewood aboard. Some of the crew left the ship and Fargo peered at those passengers who remained aboard and watched from the deck. He was beginning to think he'd done a lot of riding for nothing when he spotted the two figures on the second deck, the rat-faced one called Jimmy and one of the other men, chewing on cigars. His eyes swept the boat again but they were the only two he saw until the wood had all been loaded and the *Missouri Belle* was preparing to sail again. Suddenly Willie appeared, spoke to the other two, and all three moved down the second deck. They stopped amidships and went into the cabin area where he could no longer see them.

Dark was closing down over the waterfront as he saw dockhands tossing mooring lines back onto the vessel. He watched the *Missouri Belle* slowly drift away from the dock and the stern paddles begin to move, slowly at first, gathering speed quickly to churn the water into a white froth. It was nearly dark when the river boat began to nose upriver and Fargo left his hiding place, returned to the Ovaro, and climbed onto the horse. He rode northward, again paralleling the river, but as dark descended he moved closer to the water. He spurred the pinto into a fast trot and left the river boat behind as the craft moved slowly and cautiously along the dark, night waters. He continued to ride hard and glimpsed a haze of light back from the curving shores of the river. He made for it and found a small town, rode through it, and found it had what he wanted, an inn and a public stable.

He paid the stableboy and put the Ovaro in a roomy stall, took his heavy-weather oilskins from his pack, and set out on foot. He left the town and settled into his long, loping pace, crossed through trees and brush, climbed a low rise and then down the other side as the land began to slope to the river. When he reached the shore he halted, stripped down to nakedness, and wrapped his clothes inside the oilskins. He dropped to one knee and waited. It wasn't long before he saw a haze of light moving toward him along the river. The haze soon became the river

21

boat, the cabin areas ablaze with light, the bow and stern areas darker.

She looked almost unreal, a shimmering fantasy of light against the night. Fargo sank into the river, holding the oilskins in one hand as he began to swim out to mid-river. He halted, treading water, as the *Missouri Belle* came slowly toward him. As the heavy prow neared and he heard the thumping churn of the paddle wheel he moved to his left, watched the low forward deck slide past him, and kicked forward as he spotted a length of rope hanging down from a capstan. He grabbed hold of it, tossed his oilskins on the deck, and pulled himself up onto the vessel. He lay flat, listening to the sound of voices from amidships, and then lifted his head and peered up at the pilot's house. He glimpsed the dark outlines of figures at the wheel but no one had come rushing down to the foredeck. He made his way to where the wood was stacked, undid the oilskins, and dressed, disregarding the clamminess he felt inside the clothes.

He pushed the oilskins under a length of wood and sauntered back along the deck, nodding to a man and a woman and offering a smile to a crewman. He casually climbed an outside stairway to the second deck and spied a busboy. "Gaming room open?" he inquired.

"Yes, sir, end of the deck," the boy said, and Fargo sauntered toward the rear of the deck where the sounds of laughter and men's and women's voices grew louder. He found the gaming room, six dice and card tables and a bar. It was crowded but he stayed at the edge of the doorway, his eyes moving across the figures at the tables. Fargo figured it wouldn't be like Willie and the others to spend all their time in a cabin, and once again he found he had guessed right. Jimmy, the rat-faced one, rolled dice at one of the tables. He was losing, Fargo saw, as he stepped back from the doorway to wait.

It was not a long wait. Jimmy left the gaming room on short, hopping steps. Fargo stayed back and watched the man go down the corridor to enter a cabin door. On long strides, Fargo reached the door and saw the curtain drawn over the cabin window. It was the last piece of proof he needed. It hadn't been a wild goose chase. Thoughts raced through his mind. He had to cut down the odds and do it quietly. Sending the ship into a turmoil could backfire. He had sneaked aboard and he had no proof of anything to show a skeptical ship's master. His thoughts broke off as voices grew louder from inside the door and he ran down to the rear of the corridor, wedged himself behind a post, and saw two figures come from the room, Jimmy and the short, fleshy-faced man. They started to come toward him and Fargo edged backward, spying the stairway leading to the lower deck at the stern of the ship. He walked to it, the two figures moving along behind him, and he halted, one foot on the top step. He decided to be bold and turned to face the two men moving toward him.

"Remember me?" He smiled and saw both their jaws drop. He spun and raced down the stairs as he heard Jimmy's voice.

"Get Willie," the man said, and Fargo smiled, Jimmy's reaction exactly as he thought it would be. He reached the lower deck and saw Jimmy starting down the stairs after him. Fargo darted sideways, skirted the stern wood cords and dropped behind the stack. The thin figure came into view, moving cautiously along the stern deck. He had a gun in hand, Fargo noted as he closed his fingers around a length of firewood. He moved forward in a crouch, the piece of wood in his hand, waited till Jimmy had his back to him, and darted forward, swinging the length of wood with all his strength. It struck Jimmy across the back of the neck and he pitched face down on the deck, the gun falling from his fingers. Fargo scooped the gun into his hand and started to pull the inert form to the edge of the low deck.

But the night was still quiet and he spotted two crewmen on the low, narrow deck amidships. They'd hear the sound of a body going into the river and instantly know it for what it was. They'd probably think a passenger had fallen from the second deck, but they'd come running. Fargo turned, dragged Jimmy's body to the stern, picked it up, and flung it over the stern gunwale. It landed on the paddlewheel and was instantly pitched into the water by the giant, revolving blades whose noise covered up any sound. Fargo ducked down as he spotted the heavy-jawed figure coming down the staircase, the fleshy-faced man behind him and the third one following. Fargo stayed on one knee and watched Willie and one of the men start down the port side of the riverboat, the fleshy-faced one taking the starboard side.

He let them almost reach the bow before he leaped up and raced up the staircase, jostling two men in the corridor as he ran to the cabin. He tried the door, found it locked, and drew his leg up and kicked forward with all his strength. The door flew open and he stumbled into the room. The young woman, still bound and gagged, sat on the floor in one corner and he saw her eyes widen in recognition. He knelt beside her, pulled the gag from her face, and saw a full-lipped, wide mouth. "You," she gasped. "How did you find me?"

"We can talk later," he said, and drew the double-edged throwing knife from its calf holster around his leg to sever her bonds. "Let's go," he said, pulling her to her feet.

"My things," she said and grabbed for a leather traveling bag. "I haven't anything else," she added as she went with him, bag in hand. He ran down the corridor with her, toward the bow this time.

"They're searching the ship for me," he said as he climbed down the forward staircase with her and drew her to the bow where the shadows were darkest. "Undress. We have to go over the side," he said as he poked into the cords of wood and came out with the oilskins. He turned to her and saw she hadn't moved. "What're you waiting for, dammit?" he hissed.

"I'm not going to take my clothes off," she said.

He fastened a harsh eye at her. "I didn't come all this way for you to be modest," he growled.

"Modesty's not something you can just turn off," she protested.

"Put it this way, honey. You can be modest or you can be murdered," he said, laid the gun on the deck, and began to strip the clothes from his body. She watched him, blinking, but her eyes moved across his smoothly muscled form. He wrapped his things in the oilskins, picked up the gun, and glared at her. She still hadn't moved, emotions racing through her he saw, mirrored in her eyes. Suddenly the decision became past debating as he heard Willie's voice.

"There he is. Jesus, he's got her with him," the voice cried out, and Fargo spun to see the three figures racing toward him.

"Shit," he muttered, reached back with one hand, and sent the young woman flying over the gunwale. She screamed as she went over, the scream cut off as she hit the water. But Fargo had dropped to one knee and his finger yanked the trigger back, four shots, the gun moving only a fraction of an inch with each. The heavy-jawed man fell first, pitched onto the deck, and rolled over. The other two went down, almost at each side of him, twitched, and lay still. But the shots had resounded through the *Missouri Belle* and Fargo saw men leaning from the pilot house while other crewmen came running down both sides of the vessel. He paused, glimpsed his Colt in the big-jawed man's belt, and ran forward to yank the gun free while he discarded the other revolver.

"Stop. You, there. Stop," someone shouted, but Fargo was diving off the side of the ship, the oilskins and his Colt in one hand. He cleaved the water almost soundlessly, swam a half-dozen feet below the surface, and then rose. Shouts were coming from the river boat but he caught the sound of splashing and saw the young woman having a hard time with her clothes wet and the traveling sack in one hand. He came alongside her, closed a hand around her arm and guided her toward the shore with him. He glanced back and saw the river boat steaming onward with untouched majesty. Reaching the bank, he pulled himself ashore, helped the woman clamber out of the water and let her lay gasping for breath for a few moments. She lifted her head finally, shook herself, and sent sprays of water flying.

The night was warm but he saw her shudder. "Got anything dry to put on in that bag?" Fargo asked, and she nodded. "Go change," he said, and she rose, took the bag, and started for a cluster of hackberry. But not before she cast another glance at his naked, muscled body. He unwrapped his own clothes, tied the oilskins together again, let the night air dry him a little, and dressed. She finally came from the trees wearing a white, scoop-necked blouse and a black skirt and he had a chance to take her in for the first time. He saw a young woman of medium height, brown hair pinned atop her head, light-brown eyes, and a round-cheeked face, more wholesomely attractive than pretty, with dark eyebrows and a small nose. But her mouth was sensuous, her lips red and full, a mouth not at all in keeping with the wholesome rest of her face.

Nicely full breasts pressed against the blouse, and he saw a short waist and ample hips. "Let's walk," he said. "I know where there's an inn waiting for us."

"God, I'd like that. They kept me tied almost all of every day. Every muscle in my body hurts," she said.

"Start talking, Bess Darby," he said, and she cast a glance of surprise at him. "The desk clerk in Council Bluffs gave me your name. Now what the hell is this all about?"

"I don't know," she said, as she walked beside him and he halted to stare at her.

"I've chased you all this way, almost been shot a half-dozen times and you don't know?" He frowned.

"That's right. I don't know who they were or why they took me," she said.

"I'll be a two-headed snake," Fargo bit out.

2

"Let's try that again." Fargo frowned. "You don't know who they were or why they took you."

"That's right," Bess Darby said.

"Why are you here, or don't you know that either?" Fargo asked.

"I know why I'm here," she snapped back.

"You want to share that with me while we walk?" Fargo tossed at her.

"I'm on my way to the Black Hills to find out what happened to my father," she said.

He shot a sharp glance at her. "How do you know anything's happened to him?"

"I don't know, not exactly, but I'm afraid something has," Bess Darby said.

"Council Bluffs was an overnight stop for you?" he asked.

"Yes. I was going on by carriage to connect with the stage at Sioux City and take it from there to Black Hills Junction," Bess Darby said.

"When those gents turned up at your hotel room."

"That's right," she said, and when Fargo helped her climb a short, steep rise he saw the black bulk of the few buildings of the town come into sight.

"We'll talk more later," he said, and hurried on to the dark and sleeping town. He found the inn he had taken note of at his first visit and a small man with

28

horn-rimmed spectacles looked up from the front desk as they entered. "Two singles, next to each other," Fargo said, and the man handed him two keys. Bess Darby paid him before Fargo could get his money out, then she followed him to the two rooms. She entered the first one and he stepped in with her and took in a small room with a single bed against one wall near the lone window, a frayed stuffed chair, and a chipped bureau with a nightstand and a bowl of water atop it.

Bess sank down on the edge of the bed and suddenly her face showed worry and weariness, the round cheeks somehow drawn. "I'll have to replace some of the clothes I left in Council Bluffs," she said. "But first I'm feeling both guilty and grateful about you getting into this."

"Forget the guilty part. It just happened," Fargo said.

"I can't, and I won't forget the grateful part either," Bess said.

"Then satisfy my curiosity. How come they were waiting for you at Council Bluffs?" Fargo queried.

"I wrote my father that I was coming. Somebody either intercepted the letter or got to see it and decided to stop me. But I didn't give the route I'd take."

"That wasn't hard to figure. Most folks traveling to South Dakota would be stopping at Council Bluffs, whether they came by land or river."

"All this makes me even more worried that something's happened to my father," Bess said. "Look, it's plain I'm going to need some help. I'd like to hire you to come with me. This whole thing is becoming stranger and stranger. Here I am hiring you and I don't even know your name."

"Fargo. Skye Fargo," he said.

"Would you help me? I've the money to make it

worth your while. Thank God they didn't take that. But they clearly weren't interested in money."

Fargo thought for a moment. He hadn't any other jobs waiting and it was plain Bess Darby was into more than she could handle. "Seeing as how I've already been pulled into this, you've a deal," he said. In a moment of enthusiasm she rose and flung her arms around him, and he felt the soft touch of her breasts against his chest.

"Thank you so very much," she said, and quickly stepped back. He saw the tiny circles of color that had come into her round cheeks. "I'm sorry. I'm just so grateful."

"Anytime," he said. She returned a shy little smile and he decided she was a strange combination of timidity and determination. "But you still haven't told me why you think something may have happened to your pa," he said.

She reached into her travel sack, pulled out a folded piece of paper, and handed it to him. He sat down as he read the somewhat scrawly handwriting:

Dear Bess,
    Sorry it took so long to answer your last letter. You said you might visit. I'd like that. I'm getting worried here. There's a lot you don't know about the Black Hills Mining Company that I'll tell you when you get here. Let me know if and when you're going to visit.

                        Your Pa, Sam Darby

"I wrote asking him when he wanted me to come visit and I never heard back. That's when I began to get really concerned and I wrote again telling him about when I'd be arriving," Bess said.

"And you've no idea why someone wouldn't want you visiting your pa," Fargo said.

"Not a one," Bess answered, and he returned the letter to her.

"Let me sleep on this," Fargo said. "I don't expect any more trouble but I'll be next door. Yell if there is. I'll hear you. The walls are thin in these claptrap places."

She nodded and he went to the next room, undressed, and stretched out across the bed. He let himself ponder until sleep swept over him. The morning sun woke him and he washed and dressed and went outside and knocked on the door of Bess's room. She answered in a tan shirt and a tan skirt, her sweet, round-cheeked face looking very demure, except for that full-lipped, sensuous mouth. She was as strange a combination outside as she was inside, he decided.

"I'd like some breakfast, and then I'll try to find a store where I can replace some of the clothes I left behind," she said.

"We'll find breakfast but this town doesn't have the kind of store you'll want. You can do your replacing when we get to Sioux City to pick up the stage before you go on."

She gave him a sidelong glance. "You make it sound as if I'll be going on alone," she said.

"You will be, from Sioux City, as if nothing has happened. I'll be in the background, for the start anyway," he said. They left the room and were pleasantly surprised to find the inn serving a breakfast of eggs, bacon, and coffee. Fargo finished first, left Bess to linger over her coffee, and fetched the Ovaro from the public stable.

"I was wondering how you planned on getting to Sioux City," Bess said when he appeared.

"Two can ride as cheaply as one," he said. "We won't need to hurry and this is a fine, strong horse."

"He certainly is," she said as he helped her into the saddle and swung on behind her. "I've never ridden an Ovaro before," she said as she took in the horse's glistening white midsection and the gleaming black fore- and hindquarters. His arms pressed lightly against her as he reached around her to hold the reins and he felt the soft swell of the sides of her breasts. She smelled faintly and deliciously of lavender powder.

"You ride a lot of other horses?" Fargo asked as he sent the Ovaro northward. "Where do you hail from, Bess Darby?"

"Indiana, near Shelbyville. I had a good-paying job as a nanny for two children of a wealthy family. I'd take the kids to riding lessons at a fancy riding academy and I got to ride some of their fancy horses. Your Ovaro has a softer ride."

"That's because of good muscle and a solid frame. He's made for distance, not show," Fargo said. As if to prove his master's words, the horse took a steep incline without drawing a laboring breath or disturbing his riders. "How come your pa worked for the Black Hills Mining Company?" Fargo asked.

"On account of Pa got tired of chasing veins that didn't pan out. He was always a dreamer, trying to get rich. I always understood him better than Ma did," Bess said. "After Ma died he wrote me that he had this real good offer to work for the Black Hills company and he was going to take it. Everything seemed fine until that last letter I got."

"You just up and left your job?" Fargo asked as the Ovaro made good time across a long, flat plain.

"I gave them plenty of notice and I can always

get another job when I go back," Bess said. "If I go back."

"Not much call for nannies out here," Fargo told her.

"I suppose not," she said, and fell silent. He increased the Ovaro's pace and it was midafternoon when they reached Sioux City. They found a dress shop where Bess picked up the things she wanted, along with a new suitcase, while Fargo stopped in at the stage depot.

"We're running in luck," he told her when he returned. "The stage to Black Hills Junction only comes through once a week but it's due before sundown. I bought you a ticket."

"Good."

"The stage stops for half an hour to change horses. If there's no room you get your money back on the ticket," Fargo said, and Bess pressed a roll of bills into his hand. "It didn't cost that much," he said.

"Half your pay now, unless you want it all," she said.

"Half's fine," he said. "Let's wait at the depot." He walked to the waiting room with her, a space equipped with one long bench and a desk for the depot master. "Something's been pushing at me and I want to talk about it before you go on," Fargo said as he sat beside her on the bench. "I keep wondering about those men at Council Bluffs."

"Wondering what?"

"If they were supposed to stop you from visiting your pa, why didn't they just do it? Why were they taking you someplace?"

Bess frowned back. "Maybe they had orders to bring me someplace and find out how much Pa had written me," she ventured.

33

"Maybe so," he agreed. "And maybe something else."

"What?"

"There have been a number of young women kidnapped and sold across the border in the Canadian territories. They don't take saloon girls, only young women like you," Fargo told her.

"You saying it had nothing to do with Pa's letter and my coming out here?" Bess questioned.

"I'm saying we can't rule that out."

"I can," Bess snapped. "That'd be too much of a coincidence. They were out to stop me from getting to Pa."

Fargo shrugged and decided not to argue further. She was certain of her convictions and he was certain of nothing. But his questions had drawn a faint pout from her as she sat beside him and he was glad for the arrival of the stage. He rose as he heard it clatter to a halt outside, and stepped to the window to see that the vehicle was one of the larger, heavy Concord coaches, drawn by a six-horse team and able to hold nine passengers inside and more on the roof. But only four passengers climbed from it, the first a tall man with a long face and straight nose, wearing a gray businessman's suit, followed by a smaller man in a tailored tan jacket. The last two to step down wore cowhand work outfits, and they all followed the tall man into the depot. The driver, a gray-bearded old timer, was the last to enter the depot.

"Howdy, Zeke," the depot master greeted him. "Got one more passenger for you," he said, and gestured to Bess.

Zeke glanced at the tall man in the gray suit at once. "Depends where she's going. We're skipping some of our usual stops," the driver said. "This is

Mister Darnville. He's paid extra to get to Black Hills Junction in a hurry."

"Black Hills Junction? That's where I'm going," Bess spoke up, and the gray-suited man executed a bow.

"Albert Darnville, at your service, ma'am," he said, and gestured to the man in the tan jacket. "This is my personal assayer, Robert Dodd. These other gentlemen are my personal guards."

"Bess Darby," Bess said, and smiled.

"Don't tell me you're going to the Black Hills Mining Company, too," Darnville said.

"That's exactly where I'm going," Bess said.

Darnville's smile grew expansive. "The world is full of coincidences. Now why would a lovely young lady such as yourself be traveling to an old mining company?"

"To visit my father. He works there," Bess said.

"Well, you might be traveling with your father's new boss." Albert Darnville laughed and Fargo saw Bess's eyebrows lift. He felt his own move upward, also.

"You're going there to buy the mine?" Bess questioned.

"I'm going to make an offer if my assayer's verdict is the right one," Darnville said.

"You seem to be in a hurry to get there," Bess observed.

"Want to get there before Chet Beamer," Darnville said.

"A rival buyer?" Bess asked.

"Chet Beamer's a man with poor judgment and no principles but a whole lot of money," Darnville said, his voice growing dark.

"Sounds as if you've tangled with him before," Bess said, and Fargo silently admired the way she was drawing out Darnville.

"He's been a damn thorn in my side for years. He hasn't the business sense to know what to buy or when to buy so he watches me. When I make a move to buy something he rushes in with all his money and steals things out from under me," Darnville said with anger coming into his voice.

"You think he's on his way to the Black Hills, too?" Bess asked.

"You can bank on it. He's learned that Black Hills Mining has sent an offer to buy. There are few secrets in the financial world. By now he's on his way to make his own bid. But he'll hang back and wait to see if I make one. He won't trust his own judgment," Darnville said, and his eyes went to the big man with the lake-blue eyes standing by. "You traveling with Miss Darby, big man?" he questioned.

"No. Miss Darby and I met earlier but I'll be going on alone," Fargo said.

The driver reappeared in the doorway. "Teams are all changed. We're ready to roll," he said, and Fargo glanced outside at the gathering dusk.

"You plan to be traveling by night?" Fargo asked the driver with some surprise.

"For a little while. I know the road that goes up into the low hill country, at least the first part of it. I figure we can get in at least three hours of traveling," Zeke said.

"Everything helps," Darnville put in, and stepped aside as Bess took her bags and started from the depot. She shot Fargo a quick glance as she stepped into the stage, and he reassured her with his eyes. He watched Darnville and the others climb into the wagon and let them start off before he went to the Ovaro. He followed at a distance until darkness fell and then sent the Ovaro up on higher ground. He was riding above and across from the road when the half-moon came up and he saw the dark shape of the stage moving slowly. Fargo sent the Ovaro forward over a low hillock and took in the moonlight on the low hills that bordered the road.

He had ridden perhaps another thousand yards when he caught sight of the small knot of horsemen atop a hill. Seven, he counted. They were watching the road and he saw them start to turn away when the sound of the coach and horses drifted through the night. They instantly brought their horses back and one moved forward to peer down at the road. Fargo reined to a halt, a furrow stabbing into his brow. The stage came in sight and he saw the seven horsemen begin to move down the hill, one wearing a flat-topped hat leading the others.

They moved toward the stagecoach on the road below and Fargo watched them break into two groups. He urged the Ovaro a few steps closer as he drew his big Sharps rifle from its saddle case. But he waited. There was plenty of time for shooting. This was still a time for watching. He laid the rifle across the saddle in front of him as his gaze followed the two sets of riders as they came up on the coach from behind. Suddenly putting their horses into a gallop, they raced the few dozen yards and were alongside the coach in seconds. The guard next to the driver tried to bring his rifle around but a shot exploded and he pitched from the wagon seat. Fargo swore softly as the driver reined to a halt.

"Get down," Fargo heard the one with the flat-topped hat order as he brought his horse around. The others had their guns trained on the coach from both sides as the driver climbed to the ground. "Everybody out," the man called. Darnville emerged first, his hands in the air, followed by his assayer, then his two personal guards, and finally Bess stepped out. Fargo moved another dozen feet closer but stayed on the high ground. "Look at what we got here," one of the attackers said of Bess while the others murmured approval.

"Search them. Take their guns, first," the leader barked. Fargo continued to frown as he watched the men dismount and begin to take guns, wallets, and traveling bags from their captives and the stagecoach.

"We hit paydirt, boss. They're all carryin' a bundle, the little lady included," one of the men said as he emptied Bess's purse. He and the others gave the money to their leader, who pushed it into a money belt he wore around his waist. They herded Darnville and the other men into a huddle.

"We'll be taking the stage," the boss man said, "and the girl." Two of the men immediately seized Bess and started to push her into the stage. She hit one across the face, kicked the other, who let out a yelp of pain, and tried to run but two of the others grabbed her. One sank a blow into her stomach and she bent in two with a gasp of pain. They threw her into the stage and went inside with her. "You two stay inside with her. We don't want her jumpin' out and breakin' her pretty little neck," their leader said. "I'll drive. The rest of you bring the horses." He swung from his mount onto the stage, climbed onto the driver's seat, and took up the reins. Darnville and the others looked on, unhappy and helpless.

Fargo's eyes narrowed. One driving, two inside the coach with Bess. That left four riding alongside the coach as it began to roll forward. Fargo brought the rifle to his shoulder, remembering the ruthlessness with which they'd shot down the stage guard. He had seen enough. His finger pressed the trigger and fired two shots so rapidly they seemed one. Two of the riders toppled from their horses. A third one wheeled in a half-circle and peered up at the hillside. The shot caught him full in the chest and he flew backward over his horse's rump. But the leader was cracking a whip over the team and the wagon careened around a curve on two wheels.

The last remaining outside rider raced alongside as Fargo sent the Ovaro down the hill at a full gallop. He reached the road and glimpsed the astonished expression on Darnville's face as the Ovaro hurtled past him after the stage. Fargo rounded the curve, the coach directly ahead of him, the driver racing the horses with reckless abandon. The Ovaro closed ground and, dropping the horse's reins, Fargo brought the rifle up, aimed, and fired. The man riding alongside the coach flew sideways from his saddle as the heavy slug tore into him. The two men inside the stage were leaning out the windows and firing, but the bouncing, rolling coach caused their shots to go wild. Drawing nearer, Fargo pushed the rifle back into its saddle holster and drew his Colt.

He wanted to bring down the driver but as he closed he realized that was too dangerous, with the six horses racing at full speed and the rear of the coach skidding and bumping from side to side. No experienced stage driver, the bandit leader was having problems hanging onto the teams, yet he still had some small measure of control. Fargo holstered the Colt, realizing that if he brought down the driver the six horse team would be in full runaway. They'd surely smash the coach into a tree or rock. Staying low in the saddle, he sent the Ovaro at the rear of the big Concord coach, racing in a straight line. The two men inside continued to fire off wild shots as he reached the end of the vehicle. Fargo manuvered the Ovaro as close as he dared to one of the furiously spinning rear wheels, tightened his powerful thigh and leg muscles as he rose in the stirrups, and leaped from the horse.

He had measured speed and distance and landed inside the rear boot of the stage, grabbing hold of the leather sides of the boot to avoid being tossed out. Grateful that there were only a few suitcases inside the heavy leather enclosure that formed the boot, he clung for a moment, then reached up to the black iron strut that hung down from the roof railing where extra passengers could sit. With his hands curled around the length of iron, he pulled himself up and out of the boot, squirmed over the roof rail, and almost pitched from the coach as the rear wheels bounced over a rock. The man at the reins was still unaware of him, all his concentration focused on controlling the racing horses, and Fargo moved forward across the roof of the coach. He clung to the iron railings as he clambered over them and was almost at the driver's seat when he lost his footing for a moment. His knee hit against a corner of the rail and he swore in pain.

The driver turned, surprise flooding his face, and Fargo saw him yank the gun from his belt, still clinging to the reins with one hand. Fargo kicked out as he hung onto the roof rail, a backward kick that struck the man full in the chest. The driver fired but the shot went wild and Fargo saw the man lose his balance, his arms flailing as he went backward over the front of the driver's seat. The wheels of the coach bounced as they ran over his body and Fargo, half-diving and half-crawling, caught hold of the flapping reins. Holding them with both hands, he turned his body around and slid onto the driver's seat as his arms and shoulders instantly felt the pull of the racing horses. They were almost out of control, and Fargo held the one set of reins in his hand as he pulled back on the brake lever. The burning smell of metal against wood came to his nose and his shoulder muscles cried out as he held the brake lever hard against the spinning wheels.

The heavy stage began to slow, the horses slackening their headlong flight. He kept the brake on, forced his muscles to stay tight, and used his other arm to pull back on the reins. The coach slowed further as it rounded a long curve and he could feel the horses relaxing through the pull of the reins. Keeping a steady, firm pressure on the teams, Fargo brought the horses to a trot, then a walk, and finally to a halt as they filled the night air with deep snorting breaths and the slapping sound of tossing heads. Fargo dropped the reins and yanked the Colt out, whirled in the driver's seat, and flattened himself against the roof of the stage. He had the six-gun in place and aimed as the two men spilled from the coach. As he'd expected, they were dragging Bess with them. But his shot slammed into the first man just as he emerged and the man flew backward, his hand pulling away from Bess. His shirt was turning red before he hit the ground.

The second man let go of Bess, whirled, and raced back along the side of the stage and around the rear of the wagon. Fargo listened to the sound of him crashing through the trees in headlong flight and he holstered the Colt and swung down from the coach to find Bess Darby instantly against him, trembling. He held her till the trembling ceased and she stepped back. "Thank you," she said. "Saving my neck seems to be becoming a habit for you. It's one I certainly appreciate."

"It's one I can do without," Fargo muttered, holding the coach door open. "Get in. We'll go back and pick up the others." He climbed up on the coach to

41

take the reins again as Bess pulled the stage door shut behind her. He walked the team along the road until he found a space wide enough to let him turn and continued to keep the horses at a walk as he drove back along the road. The small, straggly group of figures finally came into sight, rushing to the sides of the road at first, then halting as they recognized the big man driving, his Ovaro trotting alongside.

"Good God, how did you bring this off?" Albert Darnville gasped out.

"Clean living," Fargo said.

"Try clean shooting," Bess said as she stepped from the coach.

"I never thought I'd see this stage again," Zeke said as he climbed up onto the driver's seat. "There's an overnight way station five miles on. That's where I was headed when they attacked."

"Find a spot to turn the coach around and come back for us," Darnville told the driver, and then turned his attention to Bess and Fargo. "I told you that Chet Beamer would stop at nothing."

"You think he's behind this attack?" Bess frowned.

"Of course. After we walked to the way station we probably couldn't get another stage for days, perhaps a week. By then, he'd be at the Black Hills Mining Company," Darnville said.

"But if he wanted you out of the way why didn't he give those varmints orders to shoot you?" Fargo questioned.

"Because you've got to understand the way Chet Beamer operates. He doesn't want me out of the way, not yet. He wants to get there first to position himself to be a bidder. That way they won't just up and sell to me. Then he'll wait for me to arrive and watch to see what I do before he makes his next move. He's as clever as he is unscrupulous," Darnville said.

"Can we get to that way station? I'm exhausted," Bess said as the stage reappeared and rolled to a halt.

"Of course, my dear. Forgive me for carrying on so about Chet Beamer, but I'm not going to let him get the best of me again," Darnville said, and walked to the stage. Bess held back for a moment.

"We'll talk later," she whispered to Fargo. He nodded and walked to the Ovaro. He rode beside the stage where the road permitted and close behind it where it didn't. It was late-night when they reached the way station, a long, low-roofed building with eight rooms. The station master, a grey-bearded man, was quick to show his gallantry for Bess.

"Our best room for the young lady," he said, and ushered her to a room that differed from the others only in that it held a chair as well as a cot.

"I'll wait for you," Bess murmured to Fargo as she passed with her traveling bag. Fargo went outside, unsaddled and fed the Ovaro, and knew it wouldn't be a long wait before the others found sleep. When he knocked softly at Bess's door, the station was a silent, sleeping place, and she opened it at once, wearing a blue nightdress that buttoned demurely to the neck yet couldn't entirely hide the soft curves of breasts and hips. "It's obvious that Darnville doesn't know the real reason those men attacked the stage. I see no need to tell him," Bess said.

"The real reason? And what would that have been?" Fargo queried.

"To do what the first ones didn't do—stop me from reaching the mine. They were backing up the others. Isn't that obvious?"

"Not to me," Fargo said blandly, and she frowned at him.

"You believe Darnville's explanation?" Bess asked.

"No."

"Then what do you believe?"

"They were a pack of bandits, plain, old-fashioned highwaymen. They probably always watched the road for the late stage. They weren't out to delay Darnville. They were out to rob him, which is exactly what they did," Fargo said.

"Then why did they take the stage?" Bess questioned.

"A Concord coach fetches a real good price. All it takes is a new coat of paint for somebody else to use it," Fargo told her.

"Then why did they take me?" she persisted.

"I think you can answer that one for yourself," he said with some irritation.

She frowned for a moment. "I think that's too much of a coincidence. First those men in Council Bluff and now these, both making off with me."

"Some men steal a chicken to eat it, some to sell it," he said.

"You're so flattering," she said with a sniff.

"You got the point."

"I still think they were after me. That was their real reason," she insisted.

"Your privilege, honey," he said.

"If you're going to work for me, it seems you ought to have more confidence in what I think," she said, and he saw that the pout had returned. Bess didn't like being disagreed with, he decided.

"I'll try harder next time," he said, and started for the door. She followed, paused as he put his hand on the knob, and suddenly her arms were around his neck, her lips gentle against his for a brief moment before she pulled back.

"Thanks for everything," she said. "Good night." She watched him leave, her eyes round and grave, but the echo of the pout was still there, he saw, and smiled to himself.

3

When morning came and the stage prepared to leave, Fargo found a moment alone with Bess. "You go on. I'll be seeing you," he said.

"Where are you going?" she said, frowning.

"Scout around some on my own."

"When do I see you again?"

"Soon enough. Maybe before you get to Black Hills Junction. Maybe not."

"I don't know if I like you just disappearing," Bess complained.

"You want me to help you or be your shadow?" he asked sharply, and her sensuous mouth edged a pout as she stepped into the coach. Albert Darnville appeared and halted before Fargo.

"I didn't thank you enough for last night, Fargo," Darnville said expansively. "I feel I ought to pay you for what you did."

"Didn't do it for money," Fargo said. "When I work for you, you can pay me."

"Well, now, if you stick around I'll keep that in mind," Darnville said, and climbed into the coach with his assayer following him. Fargo waited till the stage rolled away before he sent the Ovaro into the low hills. He watched the stage on the road below until it disappeared from sight and rode higher into the hills where he found a spot with a falcon's-eye view of the terrain below. He quickly saw the road that led from the southwest, executing a long circle before it came anywhere near the main road north. His gaze moved slowly along the rolling, lush, green land and he had just brought his eyes back to the second road when he saw the small spiral of dust in the distance. It grew larger, took shape, and became another coach moving fast along the second road. He watched it draw closer and his eyes narrowed. Not a heavy coach, but a lighter, stripped-down version often called a "mud-wagon" and more often the "poor man's Concord," its body work made of simpler joinery. It was pulled by a two-horse team.

A thought formed itself in his mind as he watched the oncoming stage below, and his curiosity made him send the Ovaro downhill along small deer trails that finally brought him to the roadway. He halted and was waiting in the center of the road as the stage rounded a curve. Fargo made out a driver and a man carrying a rifle beside him. Fargo raised one hand and saw the man bring the rifle up as the driver reined the team to a halt, glancing nervously into the trees alongside the road. Two more men leaned out of the stage, six-guns in hand.

"Easy, friends," Fargo said. "No trouble intended." Another man stuck his head out of the coach, revealing short-cropped hair and a square face, suspicion in it mixing with a belligerent arrogance.

"What do you want, mister?" the man questioned.

"Saw you coming along and thought you'd like to know there's a party of Sioux in the area, about eight if I counted their tracks right," Fargo said casually.

The suspicion faded from the square face. "Well, thanks for the warning, mister," the man said, and introduced himself. "Chet Beamer."

Fargo smiled inwardly. His hunch had proved itself right.

"You by any chance see the stage from Sioux City?" Chet Beamer asked.

"Matter of fact I did, on the main road northwest to Black Hills Junction," Fargo said.

Chet Beamer glanced up at the driver. "You see, I told you this wasn't the main road," he barked.

"They running two stages from Sioux City these days?" Fargo asked blandly.

"No, this is my private coach," Chet Beamer said. "But I'm on my way to Black Hills Junction, too, and I'm in a hurry. You know any faster way than this one?"

"The fastest way would be to hook up with the main road. You can do it a few miles north if you take the right turns," Fargo said.

"Could you show us those turns? I'll pay you for your time," Chet Beamer offered.

"Fair enough. Name's Fargo. Skye Fargo. Follow me," Fargo said, and wheeled the Ovaro around. The smile stayed with him as he rode the horse north. He was certain now that Chet Beamer had nothing to do with the attack on the stage carrying Darnville. He'd not have asked about the Sioux City stage if he had. He was simply slightly lost and running late. Putting the Ovaro into a trot, Fargo led Chet Beamer's light Concord along back trails the big Concord with six horses could never have negotiated, and finally brought them to the main road. "This is it. Stay on it and you'll end up in Black Hills Junction," he announced.

"What do I owe you?" Chet Beamer asked. "Name your price. I appreciate the help."

"Drinks next time we meet," Fargo said.

"That's mighty nice of you, Fargo. You've my

word on it," Beamer said, and Fargo watched the light Concord roll away. A lighter and faster vehicle, it would reach Black Hills Junction about the same time as Darnville in the heavy Concord, Fargo estimated, sometime in the late afternoon. It might be interesting to be there, Fargo thought, and sent the Ovaro into the low hills at a fast canter. He stayed in the hills, moving along deer and moose trails, keeping a brisk pace, and it wasn't long before he spotted Beamer's coach below. He passed it and by early afternoon he had caught up to the big Concord. He passed it, also, staying in the hills till he saw the round shapes of the Black Hills rise up.

He turned downward to the main road. The sun was in the mid-afternoon sky when he rode into Black Hills Junction. The town had grown some, he took note, busy with a goodly assortment of stores and a new bank. The saloon remained the same, its sign proclaiming it to be the Black Hills Bar and Dining Place. He took a long glance at the inn, the largest structure in town, wearing a new coat of white paint. A furrow touched his brow as he wrestled with his thoughts. He had time to kill and he wanted to visit the Black Hills Mining Company before Bess came on the scene. He always liked to take his own measure of a place or a person. Darnville and Chet Beamer were distractions, having nothing to do with Bess's purpose for coming here, he was certain. But he needed a reason to ride into the mine, he realized. He was still racking his thoughts for one when he saw a grizzled old man riding a mule laden with picks and shovels.

"How do, old timer." He smiled as he reined to a halt. "Might you know the way to the Black Hills Mining Company?"

"Follow the road out of town, turn west at the

twin rocks, and ride about half a mile and you'll come to it. But they're not hiring anybody, I can tell you that," the old man said.

"Much obliged, old timer," Fargo said, and moved on. The old miner had just given him the excuse he'd sought to find and he put the horse into a trot onto the road out of town. He found the twin rocks easily enough, two tall granite boulders side by side, turned west along a wide road, and finally halted at a sign that marked the entrance to the mine land. He paused to let his eyes sweep the low hills that rose on all sides, each with at least one mine-shaft entrance, some with as many as four. All seemed abandoned, the entrances boarded up with cross planks, rusting long toms and tools lying about.

A house lay at the foot of the largest hill, a substantial place with a low shingle roof. Four tool sheds huddled behind it and a thin column of smoke rose from the chimney. He rode to the front of the house and the door opened. A young woman stepped outside. Fargo dismounted as he took in long black hair that fell loosely around a slightly thin but beautifully patrician face, eyes the light-blue of a dawn sky, an aquiline nose, and finely-turned lips. But the light-blue eyes held a cool fire and he saw her take in his chiseled features with an appreciative appraisal. A long, deep-blue dress without a belt clung to a tall, narrow figure, long-legged, with a long shallow curve to her breasts. Somewhere in her late twenties, he guessed.

"Yes?" she asked, her voice low and cool.

"You with the Black Hills Mining Company?" Fargo asked.

"I am the Black Hills Mining Company," she said.

Fargo allowed a nod. "The world's full of surprises," he remarked. "I'm looking for work."

The cool appraisal stayed in her eyes as she took him in again with a long, careful glance. "You don't look the miner type," she said.

"I'm not," he said. "Thought maybe you might have some other kind of work."

"Such as?" she said.

He shrugged. "Anything. Payroll guard, general work, personal guard, anything. The name's Fargo. Skye Fargo."

"Sorry, Fargo, we're not hiring," the woman said.

"What is it, Linda?" a voice called out, and a man stepped from the house, medium-height, graying hair, with a thin face and quick, darting eyes, a nervous air about him instantly apparent. He looked older than the young woman, perhaps in his forties. Fargo saw the man's eyes focus on him with instant suspicion.

"Just someone looking for work, Roger," the woman said.

"We don't need anybody," the man muttered.

"You the Black Hills Mining Company, too?" Fargo inquired.

"This is my brother, Roger Ayler," the young woman said. "We run Black Hills Mining together."

Fargo pulled himself back onto the Ovaro and his lake-blue eyes stayed on Linda Ayler. "Never worked for a beautiful woman before," he lied. "It might've been fun."

Linda Ayler allowed a half-smile. "Keep hoping," she said. "You're handsome enough to be hired by one someday."

He nodded back as he moved off on the horse and heard the door close behind him. Linda Ayler had certainly been a surprise, not what he'd expected to find as head of a mining company. Roger Ayler didn't fit, either, for different reasons. There was no strength in the man, only an unsure nervousness he seemed unable to hide. The company hardly seemed in operation, either. There were questions to be answered and he found himself hoping Bess hadn't come on a fruitless search.

When he reached town he saw the two stages drawn up before the inn, their horses still drawing in deep breaths. He dismounted and hurried into the lobby. Chet Beamer and his men were at one side, Albert Darnville and his assayer at the desk, and Bess standing by. Fargo sidled over to her as Darnville finished signing in and turned to Chet Beamer. "It didn't work, Beamer. You didn't buy yourself a day for your smooth talk," Darnville said.

"I don't know what the hell you're talking about, Darnville," Chet Beamer returned.

"The hell you don't. You've no scruples and no honor," Darnville shot back.

"You just don't like losing," Beamer sneered.

"Thief," Darnville snapped.

"Fool," Beamer threw back, and Darnville turned to lead his assayer away as Beamer stepped up to the desk and signed in. "Well, didn't figure to see you again so soon, Fargo," Beamer said as he finished signing in. "Ready for that drink?"

"Not yet," Fargo said.

"You know this man?" Darnville asked.

"Yes, he was most helpful this morning," Beamer answered.

"He's the one who sent your stinking attackers running," Darnville said.

"Right now, Fargo's agreed to work for me," Bess put in.

"Seems you're everybody's little helper," Beamer commented, a slight sneer in his voice.

"Just Mister Good Samaritan," Fargo replied smiling, as both Beamer and Darnville stalked away to their respective rooms.

"What made you tell them that?" Fargo asked Bess as she registered.

"I'd have to tell them in the morning when you come along with me," she said, and he accepted the answer.

"I visited the Black Hills Mining Company," he told Bess as he went to her room with her. "Just wanted a look around for myself," he explained at her questioning glance. "The place is run by a young woman and her older brother. Seems to me they're just waiting to sell out."

"Not before they answer my questions," Bess said firmly. "Where will you be tonight?"

"Across the hall," he said.

"Good. See you in the morning," she said. "I'm very tired."

"No kiss tonight?" he inquired blandly. "Or do you only kiss when you're pouting?"

"No to both," Bess sniffed, tossed him a glare, and closed the door behind her. He went into the room across the hall, stretched out on the bed and rested for an hour, then went down to the dining room. He saw Darnville and Bob Dodd at a table against one wall, Chet Beamer and two of his men at another table against the opposite wall. He found a table in the corner, ordered bourbon and a meal and watched the others finish and leave, ignoring one another. When he finished he went back toward his room but paused at Bess's door.

"You all right in there?" he called softly, his mouth to the door.

"Yes, thank you," he heard her answer, and returned to the room across from her. He undressed and enjoyed the luxury of a good bed. The next morning, he was up, dressed, and outside before Bess appeared. She came out wearing a white shirt and riding britches, stylishly eastern-cut.

"From one of those fancy riding academies?" he commented.

"Yes," she said. "I don't want to go to the mine with Albert Darnville and I don't know Beamer. I'll buy a horse and go on my own. I'll be needing the horse to get around," she said. "Want to come along? I noticed a horse wrangler's corral at the other end of town."

"Why not?" he said. He stood by and watched as she chose a good sturdy sorrel mare with some Morgan blood in her, and Fargo saw that Bess sat the saddle with ease. "Let's go," he said, and she rode beside him as he led the way to the Black Hills Mining Company. He saw Chet Beamer's light Concord there, his three men and the driver lounging beside it. Darnville had hired a topless surrey and two of his men were alongside it. Fargo led Bess forward and through the open door of the house, hearing the raised voices as he entered the large room. Linda Ayler turned as he entered with Bess, her eyebrows lifting in surprise but her cool composure unruffled.

"I'm afraid I'm busy and we still have no work," she said.

"Found some work, for this young lady," Fargo said affably. "She's come a long way to see you."

"She'll have to wait. I happen to be busy," Linda Ayler said, and Fargo saw her brother frowning at him.

"Fargo, you do turn up at unexpected moments," Albert Darnville said.

"You know this man?" Linda asked him.

"We've met," Darnville said.

"Met Mister Beamer, too," Fargo said with a nod at Chet Beamer.

"This is becoming almost a reunion it seems," Linda said with an edge in her voice.

"Reunion? Hardly the appropriate word with that man in the room," Darnville said with a gesture toward Chet Beamer, but his eyes remained on Linda and her brother. "I've brought Bob Dodd with me. He has his assayer's equipment. If he confirms that your mine is what you say it is, I'll make you a generous offer."

"I've come all this way so you know you don't have to take his offer. You just keep that in mind," Chet Beamer put in with an almost casual disdain.

Darnville turned on him, his face reddening. "Miss Ayler and her brother are not like you. They have a sense of moral behavior. I'm sure they realize that by approaching me they made a binding offer to sell. They would recognize the ethical, moral, and legal aspects of that."

"Nonsense," Chet Beamer snorted, and focused on Linda. "Pay no attention to that. You can take anybody's bid."

"There are ethical and legal standards of behavior, not that Chet Beamer would know it," Darnville told Linda and Roger. He was working hard to see that they held on to the thoughts he wanted them to have, Fargo noted with an inward smile.

"I'm afraid we must have more time to think about all this. We had expected only Mr. Darnville's visit. This is all quite overwhelming," Linda said, and Fargo, watching her, had the feeling that it would take a great deal to overwhelm her.

"I just wanted you to know that I'll be in town and ready to make you an offer," Chet Beamer said. Darnville was right about Beamer, Fargo decided.

The man had a smooth way about him that edged on slickness. "I'll be leaving now. I'm sure I'll be hearing from you," Beamer said. He bowed, kissed Linda's hand, and strode from the room with a flourish.

"The man's completely untrustworthy. Don't think of dealing with him," Darnville said to Linda and Roger. He wasn't without his own smooth side, Fargo noted, able to hide selfish motives under an avuncular posture. "Now, when can Bob have a first-hand look at the mine?" Darnville pressed.

Linda and Roger exchanged quick glances and she left it for Roger to reply. "Whenever you like. How about tomorrow afternoon?" Roger suggested.

"Fine," Darnville agreed. "Bob will bring his equipment. See you both then." He turned and paused before Fargo. "I'll leave it to you to tell Linda and Roger about the attack on the stage Beamer arranged," he said before striding from the room.

Fargo met Linda Ayler's frowning glance. "Is that true? Did Mister Beamer have the Sioux City stage attacked?" she queried.

"Darnville thinks so," Fargo said.

Her lips pursed. "But you don't," she remarked.

"That's right," Fargo said. Her eyes went to Bess's, taking in the cool appraisal in their light-blue orbs.

"Now, what is it you want with me, Miss ... ?" she asked.

"Darby. Bess Darby. I've come looking for my father. He worked for you. Sam Darby," Bess said.

Linda tossed a glance at Roger as she answered. "Yes, he did. In fact, we're both really quite annoyed at the way he left."

"What?"

"He just up and left," Roger said. "Not a word to

55

us. Suddenly he just wasn't around, and we had a lot of work to do."

"That doesn't sound like my father. It's not the kind of thing he'd do," Bess said.

"Daughters seldom know their fathers," Linda said with cool dismissal.

"He wrote me a letter and I wrote him back. I told him I'd be coming to visit," Bess said, and Fargo groaned inwardly at her honest directness.

"What kind of letter?" Linda asked, sharpness sudden in her voice.

"Just a letter asking me to visit," Bess said, and Fargo breathed in relief. Her direct honesty had limits. "The point is, he wouldn't have just up and left unless he never got my letter," Bess said.

"We wouldn't know about that but he up and left, as you and Roger so quaintly put it," Linda said. "I can't tell you any more than that."

"I understand he lived in his own shack on the mine property. I want to look through it. Maybe I'll find something that'll explain all this," Bess said. "You must know which shack was his."

"More or less. Many of our miners had their own shacks," Roger Ayler said. "There are three hills beyond this one. Most of the shacks were between the second and third hill. You'd have to search about to find his."

"I'll do just that," Bess said. "Thanks for your time. I may have some more questions."

"I'm afraid we won't have any more answers," Linda said, and Bess turned and walked from the house. "Just a moment, Fargo," Linda said as he started to follow Bess.

"Be right there," he called to Bess as she disappeared out the door and he turned to face Linda Ayler. She was really elegantly lovely, he realized again, the light-blue eyes that were somehow cool fire, the patrician features almost classic, the long curve of her breasts just touching the white, tailored shirt she wore.

"You say you're working for that girl?" Linda asked.

"She hired me to help find out what's happened to her pa," he said.

"Whatever she's paying you, I'll pay you more," Linda said.

"Thought you said you had no work around here," Fargo remarked blandly.

"I didn't till now. I want you as a personal bodyguard. Didn't you feel the hatred in this room between Darnville and Chet Beamer? I didn't expect anything like this to happen," Linda said. "I'm sure they realize I'll be making the final decisions."

"Seems like that leaves you sitting in the catbird seat," Fargo said.

"A catbird seat that could get me killed. Whatever I decide will infuriate one of them. The one who loses might come after me, in anger or to get me to change my mind. I need someone for protection and you look like a man who can do that. I seldom guess wrong about people," Linda Ayler said.

Fargo let himself appear uncertain. "I don't know. I told Bess Darby I'd help her," he said.

"She doesn't need help. She'll just have to realize that her father took off. He was hardly a homebody. She'll just go on her way trying to find him on her own, now that she knows he's not here. You want to spend your time on a wild goose chase when you can be earning real money here?"

Fargo half-shrugged. "I've never been one for turning down a good offer. Let me think on it till tomorrow," he said.

She took a step closer to him, and the tiny flicker deep inside the cool blue eyes was definitely unbusinesslike. "You'll be much happier here. I promise you," she said softly.

"You could be right. See you tomorrow," he said, and a tiny smile touched her lips as he turned away and strode from the house.

Bess was in the saddle as he climbed onto the Ovaro. "Took you long enough," she sniffed. "You want to tell me why?"

"We can talk later," he said.

"I'm going to those hills to find the shacks Roger Ayler mentioned," Bess said.

"There's not a lot of daylight left," Fargo said with a glance at the lowering sun.

"Enough to maybe find the right shack," she said, and sent her horse up the first hill. He followed her past two abandoned mine shafts and when they rode over the second hill he saw the shacks dotting the dip between the hills. Some were only ten or fifteen yards apart, others were a good fifty yards from each other. Bess halted at the first one and dismounted. Fargo followed her inside, where he saw a mostly empty interior with a few pieces of clothing scattered about the floor. The second shack was much the same, but it held an old cardboard box. Bess turned it over and sorted through the scraps of paper that fell out. She rose to her feet after a few minutes. "These aren't any of his things," she said, and strode outside.

They had gone through five of the shacks, each containing a few items of clothing and a sack or a box that Bess examined with painstaking care, when the sun fell below the distant hills. The dusk began to descend rapidly as he walked with her to the sixth shack, some fifty yards up the hillside. He stepped inside in the last of the daylight and heard the gasp from Bess. "This is it," she said, striding across the single room to pick up a Bible lying on top of a low shelf. "This is his bible. He always carried it. Look, here," she said, opening it to the inside cover. Fargo frowned down at the initials marked there: S. D. "This was his shack," Bess said excitedly.

The interior of the shack was almost dark and Fargo found no kerosene lamps to light. "Let's go. You can come back in the morning to search the place," he said.

"I will. You can be sure of that," Bess said, and followed him to where they had left the horses. He set a brisk pace back to town that discouraged conversation and gave him more time to prepare for the moment he knew would come. Bess Darby was letting determination carry quiet fear, he realized, and that made for an inner turmoil she did a fair job of masking. But the moment surfaced when he went to her room with her. "I'm still waiting," she said stiffly. "You were going to tell me why you took so long with Linda Ayler."

"She offered me a job, as bodyguard," Fargo said, and saw Bess's eyebrows lift instantly.

"I presume you told her no," Bess said questioningly.

"I told her I'd think about it," he said, and anger came into Bess's face as her brows remained lifted.

"You'll think about it?" she echoed. "What's that mean exactly?"

"It means I think I'll take her up on it," Fargo said.

"So much for loyalty," Bess snapped, and he saw hurt join the anger in her face.

"Now, hold on," he protested, but she cut him off.

"Hold on nothing. I suppose I shouldn't be ungrateful. You did save my life. I'll make it easy for you. You're fired," she flung at him, then turned her back on him.

He pulled her around by one elbow. "Dammit, I'm doing it for you. I can find out more from inside."

"I saw you looking at her. All you want to find out is how soon you can get her in bed."

"You're sounding jealous, honey," he tossed at her.

"I'm certainly not that. I don't believe in divided loyalties. I didn't believe a word she said about Pa just up and leaving and I'm not having you work for me and for her."

"Think about it, dammit. They don't know I know about the attack in Council Bluffs. Maybe they'll let something slip," Fargo said.

"Hah! You're not even convinced about that," she threw back, and he winced inwardly. "No, I won't have it. It's just not right. You can't serve two masters."

He tried patient reasoning again, keeping his voice calm. "I told you, I'll be there for you," he said.

"That's what you say now, but it's plain you're real quick to change horses. Please leave," she said.

He swore silently. Her fury came out of fear, he knew, even if she didn't: fear that she was being abandoned, fear that she might never find the truth alone, fear that Linda Ayler might convince him that she and Roger were telling the truth. He realized he couldn't pierce her angry, racing emotions, complicated by an obviously strong sense of committment. Not now, at least. He'd give her time to simmer down, think about what he'd said, let the logic of it sink in. He drew the roll of bills from his pocket and tossed them onto the bed.

"Here's your money. No work, no pay. I've my standards, too," he said. Her glare refused to soften. "One more thing. You're being bitchy as well as dumb." He pulled back in time to avoid the slap she'd aimed at his face and left her standing with her fists clenched, the sensual mouth drawn in tightly. He hurried down the hallway and outside where he climbed onto the Ovaro.

Carl Estes
PT 25

4

The Ovaro was hidden away behind a hawthorn and Fargo lay on his stomach atop his bedroll, Sam Darby's shack in clear sight, and the dip in the ground a natural echo chamber for carrying sound. He had decided to carry through a question that had been pushing inside him. If Linda and Roger Ayler were behind the attack on Bess in Council Bluffs, Bess's sudden arrival had told them it had gone wrong. They might well decide to clear out Sam Darby's shack or get rid of it altogether. But, he thought as his lips drew back in a grimace, there was another side to the coin.

If they moved against the shack it would pretty clearly show they didn't want Sam Darby's disappearance pursued. But if there was no move against the shack it wouldn't prove they had nothing to hide. It could mean they knew there was nothing in the shack to implicate them. So he was on a kind of one-way street, yet the possible results were worth the vigil. When you sit outside a foxhole sometimes the fox comes out and sometimes he doesn't. He closed his eyes, lowered his head, and dozed in the way of the wild creatures, the senses never shut off, only put on hold.

The first sound that woke him a little over an hour later, drifting up from the base of the hills, was made by a herd of white-tailed deer. He returned to dozing and the next sound that woke him came from a pair of kit foxes squabbling. He stayed awake for a spell, his eyes on the silent shack, and when he dozed again the early dawn brought a black bear sharpening his claws against the rear wall of the shack. Fargo woke at the sound, watched the bear finally lumber away, and let himself relax for another hour, washed with his canteen, and strolled down to the shack in the morning sun. He went inside and paused. Nothing had happened during the night, nothing proven. Yet it hadn't been a waste. It had told him there could be no jumping to conclusions about Linda and Roger Ayler, despite Sam Darby's letter to Bess. And perhaps the perpetually nervous Roger Ayler knew more than his sister did.

Sunlight began to flood through the lone window of the shack and Fargo started to examine the pieces of clothing and the cardboard boxes that were still there. He was halfway through, a furrow deepening on his brow, when he heard the sound of a horse coming to a halt outside. Bess appeared in the doorway moments later, her lips opening in surprise as she saw him. "What are you doing here?" she asked. "I fired you."

"I know. I'm here on my own time. Call it curiosity. Call it wanting to know the truth. Call it whatever you like," he said, and she peered hard at him.

"You want me to hire you back?" she asked.

"No. I'm saving you money this way," he said. "Besides, you said I couldn't serve two masters, remember?"

"That mean you're still going to take the job with Linda Ayler?" Bess queried.

"That's right," he said. "That's still the best place for finding out things."

The half-pout came into her face. "You still doing it to help me?" she asked tartly, and he heard the plea under the sarcasm. He refused to make any concessions to her obstinance.

"I'm doing it for myself. You're getting a free ride," he said, and she had the temerity to look hurt, damn her. He took a small piece of paper from his pocket and handed it to her. "Here's all I've found so far. It was in the pocket of an old pair of pants. Does it mean anything to you?"

Bess stared down at the few words written on the slip of paper. "Sarah Trenchman—High Cliff Road," she read aloud. "Yes, Father mentioned her a few times in his letters. Apparently she's a woman friend of his. I remember he wrote once that she lived nearby."

"High Cliff Road," Fargo echoed. "I'll ask around. Meanwhile, finish looking through things here." She nodded and began to go through the contents of a cardboard file box while he examined the rest of the clothing in the shack. Looking under the cot, he found a pair of new Levis still in their wrapping paper. He was frowning down at the package when Bess's voice cut into his thoughts.

"Nothing in here but wage vouchers and some old receipts for mining equipment. But it's still not right," she said.

"Is that female intuition?" he asked.

"No. Pa wouldn't have gone away and not taken his Bible. He carried it everywhere he went and it's still here. If he left, he was in an awfully big hurry," Bess said.

Fargo's lips pursed. "I've been thinking the same thing for different reasons," he said. "A man doesn't leave behind a new pair of Levis and this many pieces of clothing unless he has time to grab only a few things."

"He had to run. He was afraid of something. It all fits in with his last letter," Bess said. "The Aylers have to be part of it. Who else would he be afraid of?"

"I don't know and neither do you," Fargo said. "There are things that need answers and you don't have any. Maybe the Aylers are part of it. Maybe not. Or maybe only one of them. Maybe your pa found out something about some of the other men he worked with. There are too many maybes to go around accusing anybody."

"Then I'm going to find those answers," Bess said. "I want to go through everything here again, just in case we missed something, then I'll try to find out whatever I can about Sarah Trenchman."

"I'll stop by at the inn tonight," Fargo said. "I've got to leave now."

"Of course. We wouldn't want to keep our soon-to-be boss waiting," Bess sniffed.

"No, we wouldn't," Fargo said cheerily, drawing a glare as he started for the door.

"You can tell her I'll be around with more questions," Bess called after him.

"I'll do that," he said as he left the shack, swung onto the Ovaro and rode away. When he reached the Ayler house he dismounted and went to the door and found it ajar, the voices clear from inside. Roger Ayler's came first, nervous irritation in it.

"Dammit, Linda, I didn't see any reason for you to hire that Fargo. You don't need a bodyguard," the man said.

"I think I might," Fargo heard Linda say. "It's called prudence."

"It's called twitching. I saw the way you looked at him. I know you, sister, dear."

"And you know that without me to make decisions you'd be shoveling hay someplace, brother, dear," Linda returned, sudden ice in her voice that Fargo could hear. He knew it wasn't good manners to eavesdrop but then good manners never helped find out anything.

"Uncle Phillip left me the mine, not you," Roger said with the shadow of a whine in his voice.

"Uncle Phillip always had a strange sense of humor," Fargo heard Linda toss back. He was about to put his ear closer to the open door when he heard a sound and turned to see the topless surrey coming up the road, Darnville and his assayer in it. He straightened up and knocked on the door. Linda opened it farther in a few seconds.

"Company coming," he said, and gestured to the road. "Glad I got here first."

"Come in," Linda said. She was clad in brown work trousers that she somehow managed to make look glamorous and a beige cotton shirt tight enough to outline the long curve of her breasts. "Made your mind up about my offer?" she asked him just inside the doorway.

"Seems too good to turn down," Fargo said. Out of the corner of his eye, he saw Roger turn away.

Linda's hand pressed his arm. "I'm very glad," she said. "Did you tell the little Darby girl?"

"Yes. She wasn't happy."

"She'll get over it."

"She'll probably be calling again," he said.

"Yes, I expect she will," Linda said, her hand still on his arm. "She seems quite distrustful, suspicious of everything. She ever give you any reason for that?"

"No. But then she didn't really have time to confide much in me," Fargo said. Linda shrugged and pulled her hand away as Albert Darnville appeared at the door.

"You're very prompt, Mister Darnville." She smiled graciously. "I hope that means you're anxious to make an offer."

"It might," he said, and gestured to Bob Dodd. "But that depends on what Bob tells me." Darnville's eyes went to Fargo. "Didn't expect you here," he said.

"Fargo's going to be working for me," Linda said. Darnville turned to Roger Ayler.

"Bob has all his equipment with him. Can we drive the surrey to your mine entrance?" Darnville asked.

"Of course," Roger nodded. "Let's get right at it."

"Come along," Linda murmured to Fargo, and he fell in step beside her as everyone went outside. Bob Dodd's satchels took up a lot of the space inside the surrey and there was only room for three passengers. "We'll walk," Linda said. "It's not that far."

"That's gracious of you," Dodd said as he climbed into the surrey. Fargo watched the wagon climb up the hills, moving along the narrow passages between most of the low hills, and finally climb up one long slope to the highest of them.

"How about we ride?" Fargo said, and Linda shrugged agreement and climbed onto the Ovaro in front of him. Her long, willowy body pressed back against him, soft yet firm. "All these abandoned mine shafts yours?" Fargo asked.

"All on these hills," Linda said. "That's the mining business. You sink fifty shafts, sometimes a hundred, to find one that is a strike."

Fargo followed the surrey to the top of the long hill where the mine opening rose tall and dark. As

Fargo rode to a halt, Bob Dodd was unpacking his equipment: scales, bottles of chemicals, tools, a microscope, and a large magnifying glass. Darnville helped him carry everything into the mine as Roger Ayler lighted a row of kerosene lamps down the long tunnel of rock and dirt. Dismounting, Fargo entered the mine with Linda and walked down the long corridor, halting where Bob Dodd had set up his equipment at a spot where yellow veins were clearly visible in the dirt wall. With a small pickax, the assayer began to chip off pieces of the yellow metal as Roger Ayler helped and Darnville looked on.

Fargo continued walking down the mine tunnel with Linda, slowly taking in the yellow veins he saw as he casually strolled. "You've no miners working here at all, it seems," he mentioned.

"That's right. Roger let them all go when we decided to stop operations," Linda replied.

"What made you decide to do that?" Fargo asked.

"A number of things, mostly economic. It became obvious that we'd need a lot more money than we had to develop this mine. Our best course, we decided, was to find a buyer and sell out. It really is the best solution. Neither Roger nor I are interested in mining," she said, and Fargo nodded, her answer making perfect sense. He paused at another of the yellow veins.

"It seems this is a rich vein you have here," he observed.

"It is, the only good one we've struck. We knew it wouldn't interest a buyer unless it was rich enough and we mined for over a year to make sure," Linda said, and walked close beside him as he returned to where the assayer was taking samples from another place in the mine shaft. Dodd took samples from over a dozen places before he began examining, and analyzing, using all his equipment with concentration. "This is going to take a while. Let's go back to the house," Linda said to Fargo, and he followed her from the mine.

Roger hurried after them. "I wish you'd stay, Linda," he said, his tone something between a demand and a plea.

"Don't concern yourself, Roger. Everything will be fine," Linda said.

"You don't know this man," Roger said. "Be careful."

"I intend to get to know him. I won't have anyone working for me I don't know about. Stop worrying, Roger," Linda said, and hurried on and swung onto the Ovaro. Fargo followed. The exchange had been an echo of what he had eavesdropped upon with the strange same twist to it, Roger nervously carping at Linda when it was plain she was the stronger of the two. Fargo decided to press the issue a little as he climbed into the saddle.

"Why is Roger so upset at you hiring me?" he asked casually.

"It's nothing personal, Fargo. Roger is so dependent on me he resents anyone else," Linda said. Once again, he was struck by the logic and reasonableness of her answers. He was beginning to wonder more and more if Roger's nervousness might be because he was hiding something from her as well as from the rest of the world. But he didn't press further, and when they returned to the house Linda offered him a drink of good rye whiskey.

"Never refuse a good drink. It's against my religion," he said, and took a deep draw of the rich liquid. Tiny little lights shone in the depths of her cool blue eyes as she sat across from him.

"Tell me something more about Skye Fargo so I can satisfy Roger," she said.

"Some people call him the Trailsman," he told her.

"I see," she said thoughtfully. "Which means you don't stay long in one place."

"Not usually," he said, savoring the richness of the liquor.

"Could you find new trails for me?" she asked.

"You thinking about new trails?" he questioned.

"After the mine is sold," she said. "I imagine it'd be real fun exploring with you."

"It might be," he said.

"We could find out," she murmured. "Do I surprise you?"

"Some," he said, and remembered what Roger had said to her. Perhaps Roger knew his sister's weakness and it made him nervous. Did he fear she might talk too much when she thirsted too much? Fargo wondered. But about what? He pushed aside racing thoughts to enter Linda's game playing. "Why me? If you sell the mine you'll be able to buy any man you like. Just about," he said with a smile.

"For one, just about isn't good enough. Two, I wouldn't want a man I could buy. Three, that'll be a while yet and you're here now," she said.

"A dick in hand is worth two in the bush?" Fargo remarked.

Her lips formed a sly smile. "Couldn't have said it better myself."

"Maybe you're buying me," he slid back at her.

"No, you're not the kind who can be bought," she said, finishing her drink. "You can be hired, but not bought." He smiled, not without admiration. He had learned one thing about Linda Ayler. She was not simply clever; she was smart. "How did you meet up with Bess Darby?" Linda asked.

He thought for a moment about leveling with Linda, but quickly decided against it. Too soon, he told himself. She was still too much a question mark. Everything here was too much a question mark. "By chance, in Council Bluffs," he said. "She was very shaken up. Seems she'd had some kind of incident. She never did tell me what," he said, and his eyes held on Linda over the rim of his glass. But he could detect no change in her expression. "That's when she told me she was trying to find out what happened to her pa and decided she was afraid to go on alone. She offered good money and I agreed. Her first stop was here."

"Well, we can't help her any, but she'll be fine on her own. Did she find anything at her pa's shack?" Linda asked almost off-handedly.

"Nothing important," Fargo said, and realized Linda had a way of slipping in seemingly casual questions that might be simply curiosity, or cleverness.

"Are you officially working for me, now?" Linda asked.

"Tomorrow. I haven't given Bess her money back, yet," he lied, downing the last of the whiskey.

"You'll be staying here, of course. A bodyguard ought to be close," she said.

"How close?" Fargo asked, and Linda leaned forward and he saw the tiny points press into her cotton shirt. Then her mouth was on his, lips parting at once, asking and demanding.

"This close," she murmured. She pulled back as the sound of a horse coming to a halt outside drifted into the room, the tiny lights in her eyes dancing. "Come in," she called at the knock on the door. Fargo was sitting back as Bess stepped into the room. "Miss Darby again," Linda said coolly.

"Yes, again," Bess said. Fargo noted that she pointedly avoided glancing at him. "Do you have any of my father's personal things here?" she asked Linda.

"Now, why would we have that?" Linda returned with cool reproach, and Fargo saw Bess grow flustered, tiny spots of red appearing in her cheeks.

"I thought perhaps someone might have started to clean out the shack before I arrived," she almost stammered.

Linda's cool disdain was piercing. "I told you, no one cared about his shack," she said, and the spots of red in Bess's cheeks grew larger.

"Would you know who Sarah Trenchman is?" Bess asked and Fargo swore silently.

"Never heard of her. Why?" Linda said at once. "What has she got to do with your father?"

"I don't know. Maybe nothing. But I'm going to find out. I may be back," Bess said.

"You'll only be wasting your valuable time," Linda said, and Bess spun and strode from the room, her cheeks full scarlet now. Damn, Fargo swore inwardly. She was too emotionally involved to think or act cleverly. He felt for her but kept his expression one of cool concern. Linda turned to him as Bess disappeared through the doorway. "Finish with her, Fargo. She's not worth your time," Linda said, and he shrugged, a gesture he knew Linda would take as agreement.

The sound of the surrey drawing up outside came into the room, quickly followed by the entrance of Albert Darnville, then Roger, and Bob Dodd. Darnville wore an expansive smile as he approached Linda. "Every sample Bob examined was excellent, not a single instance of fool's gold among them. I'm pleased, very pleased," Darnville said. "From the extent of the surface veins it's obvious there is a lot

72

more gold deeper down. But of course, this will require a good deal of mining and equipment and all the expenses involved in a major operation."

"Exactly why I contacted you, because we don't have the money for that," Linda said.

"Mister Darnville's going to make us an offer," Roger put in excitedly.

"Tomorrow, probably. I need some time to carefully go over the estimated costs with Bob." Darnville smiled. "But things look very promising."

"That's wonderful," Linda said, linking her arm in his as he started for the door. "You know I'll be waiting." She smiled warmly.

"One thing," Darnville said as he paused in the doorway. "You're not to tell any of this to Chet Beamer if he comes around. Our discussions are strictly confidential."

"Of course," Linda said, and brushed Darnville's cheek with a kiss. When he left she swirled back into the room and Fargo saw the triumph in her face. "What did I tell you, Roger?" she said to her brother, and then glanced at Fargo. "Roger was always afraid it wouldn't work out for some reason or another."

"It's worked out better than I'd hoped. We even have Mister Beamer in the wings," Roger admitted.

"Yes, but I'll handle that. We don't want to set off anything and we wouldn't want to do anything unethical," Linda said, and Fargo couldn't hear anything but honesty in her tone.

"I'll be going on for now," he told her, and she walked from the house with him. He paused to take in four men lounging against a fence post beside their horses. "Thought you said you'd dismissed everybody," he remarked.

"We dismissed the mine workers. Those are security. They're Roger's idea. They patrol the outer perimeter of our hills through the night."

"For what?" Fargo queried.

"Trespassers," Roger Ayler's voice answered, and Fargo turned to see him standing in the doorway. "Even abandoned mine shafts attract pack rats hoping to find a few flakes, and I don't fancy trespassers."

"I can understand that." Fargo smiled as he climbed onto the Ovaro. Linda stood beside the horse, her voice low.

"I'll be up late if you decide to come back tonight," she said.

"Good enough," he said, and rode away at a trot. He passed the four men who watched him go with expressionless eyes. Hired drifters, Fargo murmured to himself, taking in their cracked leather boots and frayed gunbelts. He rode on as the sun began to dip to the far end of the sky and it was almost dark when he reached Black Hills Junction. He halted at the bar and went inside, ordered a bourbon, and struck up a conversation with the bartender, an amiable-faced gray-haired man.

"Just passing through?" the man asked. "There's not a lot of work around here these days. Most of the mining operations are shut down."

"Why's that?" Fargo inquired.

"A lot of folks think the good gold strikes in these hills are past," the bartender said.

"I'm looking for somebody. Sarah Trenchman. You know her, by any chance?" Fargo asked.

"Sarah Trenchman? Hell, everybody in the Black Hills knows Sarah. She's delivered about every baby born around here," the man said. "She's the only midwife around and a damn good one, too. Yep, everybody knows Sarah."

"Where do I find High Cliff Road?" Fargo questioned.

"Go west from town. You'll see a place we call the pinnacle rock, a tall, pointed formation. Right behind it a steep hill goes up. High Cliff leads around it to the top where Sarah lives. The road's plenty wide enough; Sarah uses it with her buckboard all the time. But one side is a sharp, steep drop."

"Much obliged," Fargo said. He finished the drink and left with a wave from the bartender. A furrow dug into his brow as he led the pinto down the street. Linda had told Bess she'd never heard of Sarah Trenchman, yet the bartender said the woman was known to everyone. It was the first time he'd found anything Linda had said that wasn't reasonable and in order. Yet he couldn't jump to conclusions. It was just possible that Sarah Trenchman had never come to Linda's attention. He tucked the question into a corner of his mind as he reached the inn and went inside. Bess opened the door of her room at his knock, her face set.

"Sorry I disturbed you earlier. It seemed real cozy," she sniffed.

"We were discussing my duties," Fargo said. "Why'd you ask Linda about Sarah Trenchman? Ever hear of keeping things to yourself?"

Bess's cheeks grew red again. "I thought she might know who she was and I'd save time trying to find out elsewhere," she said.

"Not very smart," Fargo grunted.

"I'm new at this," she returned. "But I still don't believe her about anything."

"You can believe her about not being interested in the shack, at least not anymore. I waited outside it all night and no one showed up to make sure it didn't hold anything important," Fargo told her and

75

saw the surprise come into her eyes. "I also found out about Sarah Trenchman," he said.

"So did I," Bess said smugly.

"Where'd you ask?" he frowned.

"Around town, the general store, the stage depot, some men watering their horses at the trough," she said. "I'll be paying Sarah Trenchman a visit in the morning."

"I was thinking of doing that myself," he said. "We'll go together." He saw her hesitate, uncertainty coming into her round-cheeked face. "Spit it out," he said.

"I just don't know about your loyalty anymore, working for the Aylers. I want to believe you but I keep wondering," she said.

He couldn't be angry, he realized. She was uncertain and afraid and alone. "I can go talk to her on my own, you know," he said. "It's a free country."

"Yes, of course." Bess nodded and looked ashamed. He offered her a compromise.

"Suppose I meet you there?" he suggested, and she nodded at once, grateful to draw back on what she'd said.

"All right. I'll see you there," she said, and suddenly she was standing close to him, her brown eyes very round. "What do you think about Linda Ayler, Fargo?" she asked. "I'd like an honest answer."

"So far she's answered most everything right," he said. "I'm wondering more about Roger Ayler."

Bess frowned. "You mean you think he's behind things and she's not."

"It's possible," Fargo said. "If anybody's behind anything. We still don't know about that."

"I know, you're still not sure who sent those men after me in Council Bluffs," she said with a pout.

"That's right," he said. "And I'm not calling anybody anything until I am sure."

"You stay with your logic. I'll stay with what I feel inside," Bess said self-righteously. "Just make sure it's logic, not your loins, that convince you."

"See you in the morning," he said, and smiled to himself as he left, aware that she had a point. Outside, he stopped back at the bar and had something to eat and decided that perhaps it was time to probe a little harder at Linda, perhaps in more ways than one. He finished eating and climbed onto the pinto and turned the horse north through the night.

5

There was a light on in one room at the left side of the house as Fargo rode up, dismounted, and tied the Ovaro to a thin, lone sapling. He walked to the window and peered in, feeling not unlike a Peeping Tom. He saw a bedroom done in blue; blue curtains, light-blue walls, and a blue drape over the bed. Linda, in a white silk robe, sat at a small end table with some papers spread out in front of her. He tapped softly against the window and she turned at once, surprise in her face, then a smile came to her lips as she saw him. She opened the window for him and he stretched long legs over the sill and climbed into the room.

"What a pleasant surprise. I didn't really expect you'd come," she said.

"Thought I'd visit," Fargo said. "I didn't see any of Roger's security men."

"They mostly patrol along the far side of the hills," Linda said, and sat down at the edge of the bed. The neck of the silk robe fell open and he glimpsed the long, smooth curve of one breast as he sat down beside her.

"Spoke to Bess Darby about Council Bluffs. She told me what happened there," Fargo said carefully and Linda waited. "Some men grabbed her and tried to go off with her. She managed to get away," he went on.

"How terrible," Linda murmured. "And she immediately thought they'd been sent to stop her from coming here."

"Yes," Fargo agreed.

"How ridiculous, to say nothing of highly presumptious, of her. But it's understandable," Linda said with more sympathy than he had expected.

"That's understanding of you," he said honestly.

"I feel sorry for the poor little thing, even though I don't enjoy being suspected of God-knows-what," Linda said. "But I hope you didn't come here just to tell me that."

"No, but I thought you'd like knowing." Fargo smiled.

"Thanks," she said, and a quietly amused smile touched her lips. "What exactly did you have in mind?"

"You did the inviting," Fargo said.

"So I did," Linda said. She leaned forward and her arms slid around his neck, her mouth finding his. Her lips were open at once and her tongue darted out with demanding insistence, touched, circled, probed deeper. He pushed the silk robe open, she wriggled, and the garment fell away entirely leaving her naked before him. He took in large breasts, with a slow, shallow curve to them, but filling out at the cups, a linear loveliness to them, each tipped with a dark-brown nipple on an areola a shade lighter. A long, narrow waist followed with an almost flat belly, narrow hips, and thin, yet not without shapeliness, smooth legs. A surprisingly small black triangle fitted the long-lined body.

He felt her hands pulling at his clothes and he helped shed gunbelt and trousers, and in moments he was with her, skin against skin, and her long, thin legs rose to fold around his thighs, pull away, and rub up and down against him. Linda moved back to take in the muscled symmetry of him and her eyes lingered on the pulsating erectness that was already waiting for her. She gave a tiny gasp of anticipation and delight. Her hand closed around him, pressed, pulled, and her mouth came to his again. "Jesus ... oh, God, yes, I knew.... I knew," she breathed, and her hips were already lifting, her long body trembling. His mouth moved to trace a moist path down the long, shallow curve of her breasts, found one brown nipple, and drew it in and Linda half-screamed with delight. Her hand came to the back of his neck, pressed him down harder against her breast as he pulled on it, caressed, pulled again and she was uttering loud, groaning cries and he could feel the need gathering quickly inside her.

He moved his torso, came down across the small, black triangle, the pubic mound beneath it also small but firm. Her legs lifted and clasped around him and she was pushing upwards and he could feel the warm moistness of her flowing against him. He slid forward into the dark warmth and Linda screamed with the touch, her hands digging into his back. Her long body trembled violently as she thrust upward against him, held herself tight to him, arms wrapped around his back as she made spasmodic, short thrusting motions and he felt her tightening against him with each one. "Agh ... agh ... agh," she grunted, over and over, and her urgent sounds grew deeper and breathier as he thrust deeper and harder. "Yes, yes, yes, oh, Jesus, yes ... agh ... agh ... oh, yes," Linda gasped and cried and gasped again and now one hand encircled his neck, pressing his face down to her breasts that moved from side to side as her upper torso twisted.

Suddenly the grunts turned into a long groaning sound that seemed to come from the pit of her belly and he saw her eyes snap wide open, the cool blue now circled with blue flame. She seemed to stare unseeing at him as she lifted and rose beneath him. "Now, now, now . . . oh, God now . . ." Linda gasped out and he felt her tightness around him as he let himself release. Her scream of ecstacy circled the room, held in mid-air as though it would never end until finally, with a gasping whimper, it broke off and Linda's long body fell back with a sudden limpness. He stayed in her, still pulsating, and she made small, satisfied groans until finally she lay still, making a sound only when he pulled from her.

He lay beside her, taking in the long body and the shallow curve of her breasts, the small triangle now moist. She was all of a piece, everything flowing in long lines. She opened her eyes and half-rose to turn to him and a small smile formed on her lips. "You're back," he said, and her smile widened.

"That always happens with me at a certain point. It's like I'm in another world," she said and lay back and pulled him half-across her. "I was right about you. You're something special. I'm going to enjoy keeping you around after the mine is sold."

"What happens to Roger then?" Fargo questioned.

"He goes his way. I go mine," Linda said.

"I take it you're not all that close."

"We are in some ways. I told you, Roger is dependent on me. He resents that, of course. Money will allow him to stop being dependent on me," Linda said.

"You saying he doesn't do anything on his own?" Fargo asked, choosing his words carefully.

"He might, out of resentment. I don't know," she said, and Fargo decided to live with that answer.

"Whose idea was it to get rid of everybody working for you?" he asked.

"Roger's," she said. "He said it was stupid to keep paying them after we closed down operations. I couldn't disagree."

"I suppose not," Fargo said, and promised himself to pay more attention to Roger. Linda turned on her side and came against him.

"I'm very sleepy," she said. "Good night." She closed her eyes and in moments he heard the steady, even breathing of sleep. He swept the long loveliness of her with a slow glance. Maybe she didn't know Roger as well as she thought. Maybe Roger did a lot of things under her nose she simply didn't realize. Yet it was hard to see her as being that gullible. Linda was plainly a young woman who knew what she wanted and usually got it. She was becoming something more than a question mark; she was becoming an enigma. But a most enjoyable one, he admitted, closing his eyes and letting himself welcome sleep.

She woke when he rose with the first light of dawn, and watched him dress. "I don't think it'd be good for Roger to see me here with you when he wakes," Fargo said.

"No, it'd only upset him more," Linda agreed.

"I'll see you later," Fargo said.

"I'm sure of that." Linda smiled confidently and he went out the window to where he had left the Ovaro. He led the horse quietly away from the house and took to the saddle only when he was far enough away not to be heard. He rode slowly and scanned the hills for a sign of Roger's security patrol and found none. As he rode, the morning spreading itself over the land, he decided to give Bess some time alone with Sarah Trenchman before he came on the scene. It might be a good thing, and it would be a gesture Bess would recognize.

He found a small pond and washed, ate from a cluster of wild cherries along the way, and finally rode toward town, turned west, and found the pinnacle rock, a dark-gray basalt formation. Behind it he spied the steep hill and High Cliff Road where it began to wind its way up the side of the hill. It rose sharply and he was certain it took great care to drive a buckboard down it. The drop at one side was indeed sheer, he noted, rock covered with mountain brush, a tough and hardy growth, burdock and bracken mixed in with it. Venturing along the edge of the road, Fargo saw very thick growths of hawthorns and mountain laurel, with some rocks rising higher at the bottom of the cliffside.

Moving back to the other side, he continued on to the top of the hill where he found a sturdy cabin with two chimneys, a half-dozen poland china hogs in a pen, and two cows wandering on their own. A three-sided barn rose at the rear of the cabin, close but not attached, and beside it, a shed with the buckboard inside it. Two strong-legged horses with perhaps some Clydesdale blood in them were enclosed in another small corral. But he didn't see Bess's sorrel and he was frowning as he rode to a halt and dismounted. A woman stepped from the house, an old splint broom in one hand. Tall and large-boned, graying hair pulled back, she had a pleasant face with few lines in it, and showed strength in the angle of her jaw. He guessed her to be in her forties.

"Sarah Trenchman?" he asked.

"That's right," the woman said.

"Name's Fargo. Skye Fargo. I was to meet someone

here, a young woman who was coming to see you," Fargo said.

"No one's showed up here except you," Sarah Trenchman said. "Cup of coffee while you wait?"

"I'd like that," Fargo said, and followed her into the house where he saw two rooms, the main one a warm, cozy place decorated with Indian blankets hanging on the walls and a huge hooked rug. Comfortable chairs were arranged casually and a good oak table took up one side of the room. Sarah Trenchman took a tin coffee pot from a grill over hot coals and poured him a cup of the liquid. He took a sip and found it rich and strong.

"This young woman coming to see me about having a baby?" Sarah Trenchman asked.

"No," Fargo said.

"She have a name?" the woman asked pointedly.

Fargo smiled. "Yes, I was waiting for her to come and introduce herself. I expected she'd be here before me. Her name's Bess Darby."

Sarah Trenchman's eyes grew wide as surprise flooded her strong face. "Sam Darby's daughter?" she gasped.

"That's right," Fargo said.

"I know what she wants to ask me," the woman said. "And I can't give her the answer she wants."

"What can you give her?" Fargo questioned.

"A few things, whatever Sam told me. He was still holding back," Sarah said, and cast a quick, sharp glance at Fargo. "How do you fit in with this, young man?" she probed.

"I'm trying to help Bess get at the truth," Fargo said. "Sam Darby wrote her a letter that alarmed her and when he never answered her return letter she became frightened. She decided to come get answers for herself. Enough happened on the way to make her sure someone doesn't want her here."

Sarah Trenchman frowned into space. "I've been real worried, too, but afraid to pry too much."

"Why?" Fargo asked, puzzled.

"Because I didn't know how to begin and I was afraid I might hurt Sam more," Sarah said.

"You're not making a lot of sense, Sarah Trenchman," Fargo pointed out.

"Guess not. Maybe I'd best just tell you what I know," the woman said, and Fargo rose and peered out of the doorway, straining his ears, but he heard no sound of hoofbeats coming up the road.

"Bess should have been here by now. I don't like this. Hold what you have to tell me while I go take a look for her," Fargo said.

"It's held this long. A little longer won't make any difference," Sarah replied dryly.

Fargo hurried outside and swung onto the pinto. He sent the horse down High Cliff Road at a walk. On the way up he hadn't scanned the ground, intent simply on getting to the top, but now his trailsman's eyes searched the road. He picked up the buckboard tracks at once, and three sets of hoofprints of single riders, all of them dried and cracked and at least three days old. His eyes moved from side to side of the steep road and he was halfway down when he reined to a halt. The soil was churned, marred by the hoofprints of at least four horses, perhaps more, it was hard to tell. He let his eyes move to the cliff edge of the road as he dismounted, and he saw the long, dragging marks there. He swore as he dropped to one knee, his fingers pressing into the marks in the soil. They were new, moist, the undersoil fresh. He peered down over the steep side of the drop, his eyes narrowed, straining. He saw that the top branches of the hawthorn directly below were bent, a few splintered and broken off.

He rose, took the lariat from its strap, and surveyed the wall of earth, rock, brush, and twisted tree forms that rose up on the other side of the road. Approaching a twisting tree that grew almost horizontally out of the earth, he reached up with both hands and grabbed hold of a branch. It held his weight with only the slightest bend and, satisfied, Fargo dropped to the ground and wrapped one end of the lariat around the branch, took two half-hitches for extra strength, and stepped to the other side of the road. With a turn of the lariat around his waist, he began to lower himself over the edge.

Bracing his feet against the wall of the cliffside, he began his descent, scanning the steep but uneven side of soil and rock, and the brush, lichen, ivy, and bracken growing across it. A little more than halfway down to the bottom the side protruded perhaps a foot away from the rest of the cliff, and his lips thinned as he saw the flattened imprint where something had struck against the protrusion on its way down. He continued to lower himself, and when he reached the top of the hawthorn the broken branches became a clear outline. He paused, held himself in place, and peered down into the thick bush, cursing as he spied the form lying cradled in the low branches of the hawthorn. He lowered himself through the narrow opening of the broken branches until he reached Bess and immediately leaned his head down against her. She was unconscious but alive, her breath steady.

Working carefully so he wouldn't dislodge her from her precarious cradle, he wrapped the lariat around her and then brought the rope up to criss-cross his shoulders and chest and down to wrap around his waist. Bess lifted as he began to pull himself upward, her body coming up to fall against his back. Using his feet braced against the cliff wall once again, he pulled himself and his burden up the steep side. He hadn't reached the halfway point when his arms felt as though they were about to tear out of his shoulders. He paused, let his muscles rest for a moment, then went on. Long before he reached the top his muscles were crying out, his breathing becoming harsh. He rested more often, then pulled himself on in shorter spurts of fading strength.

The pain was all through his body, his wrists and fingers aching, Bess a totally inert weight on his back. He would have groaned in relief if he'd had the strength when the top of the cliffside came into sight. Drawing on a last burst of strength, he drew himself over the edge and fell sprawling across the road on his face, Bess attached to him. He lay prone and drew in deep draughts of air, feeling his muscles begin to uncramp. Finally, he reached back and unwrapped the lariat from around Bess and himself so he could slide forward. He turned her on her back, made sure her breathing was still regular, then rose, took water from his canteen, and sprinkled it on her face. She remained unconscious, and he put the canteen back in its place and returned to her. He examined her and saw the large red bruise on her temple, another at the back of her neck. The tan shirt she wore was ripped in a half-dozen places and he saw the scratches along her arms. His eyes went down to her wrists and hands and saw she held one hand tightly clenched.

Gently, he pried her fingers open and stared down at the torn piece of material in the palm of her hand. He held it up to examine it and saw it had been ripped from the front of a wool shirt, a button still attached. The scrap was dark red with black stripes running through it. Fargo pushed it into his pocket, realizing that Bess had put up a real fight before she was tossed over the cliff. He lifted her limp form and placed her on her stomach across the saddle. He climbed onto the horse's rump and, leaning forward to hold the reins, rode slowly up the road.

Sarah Trenchman came from the house as she saw him ride to a halt. "My God, what happened?" she asked.

"Found her at the bottom of the cliff. She's lucky to be alive," Fargo said.

"Get her inside," the woman said, leading the way into the second room where Fargo saw two cots in a nicely furnished bedroom with stacks of clean cloths and towels piled high in an open-faced case. "That one," Sarah said, motioning to one of the cots, and Fargo gently lay Bess down. Sarah Trenchman took over at once, opening Bess's shirt, listening to her heartbeat with a stethoscope, taking her pulse, and examining her bruises. "Wait outside till I finish," the woman said, and Fargo went into the main room and poured himself a cup of coffee. He had just finished the last of it when Sarah Trenchman entered from the other room. "Nothing broken, far as I can tell," she said.

"Didn't seem so," Fargo agreed.

"But she's still unconscious. She may be in a coma from shock or a blow. She's pretty banged up. I undressed her and wrapped her in blankets," Sarah said, and poured coffee for herself. "What do you think happened? Her horse shy and throw her? That's happened before on High Cliff Road. It makes horses skittish."

"She was thrown over the side," Fargo said.

"My God," Sarah Trenchman said, blanching. "You sure of that?"

"Sure enough," Fargo said.

"That's Sam's daughter, I take it," Sarah said.

Fargo nodded. "Suppose you tell me everything you know," he said.

The woman took a long sip of her coffee and leaned back in the chair. "As I said, it's not a lot. I can tell you what was bothering Sam. He told me that much but he never told me anything more. He gave me the bare facts, nothing else."

"Start with that," Fargo said.

"Sam and I became good friends when he came here to work for Black Hills Mining. He visited often and, when he had time, drove me to a delivery. He was one of seven men who came to work for the Aylers at the same time, all hired together. They worked at the mine for over a year. Sam always told me it was a special job and they were all getting really good pay. Lots of times they worked by lamplight at night, he said."

"Then what happened?" Fargo queried.

Sarah Trenchman frowned into space. "Every one of the men that worked with Sam began having fatal accidents. Ken Dillon was riding when his horse must have thrown him. He was found with a broken neck. Ed Hurvey drowned while swimming in the lake near Deadwood. Ralph Bell came back drunk one night and set fire to his shack and himself. Sam said that was especially strange since Ralph wasn't a drinking man. John Ryder was found robbed and shot to death on the road to Pine Ridge. Ben Beezman was found dead in one of the old abandoned mine shafts. Floor planking gave way under him and he dropped to his death. Nobody ever knew what he was doing there. John Masters was driving a big load of planking in the mine wagon when the ropes holding the wood broke and the whole load came down on him and crushed him to death. He was alone so nobody ever knew how the ropes gave way."

"That left Sam Darby the last one alive," Fargo said.

"And feeling very uncomfortable," Sarah said. "There were some that said there was a hex on the whole operation but Sam never believed in hexes and he couldn't understand such a run of bad luck."

"So what did he think?"

"He never said, but he was afraid, very afraid. I tried to get him to talk more but he wouldn't."

"The Aylers said he just up and left without telling them or anyone else. Is that true?" Fargo asked.

"It seems so. I never heard any more from him," Sarah said.

"Do you think he's dead, too, another accident?" Fargo probed.

"I don't know. Nobody's ever found his body, if that's what it was. I think he did up and leave and he's hiding someplace."

"Without saying a word to you?"

"That'd be like Sam. He held back, I told you."

"You have any idea where he might have gone?" Fargo queried.

"Not far. Sam had a bad leg. If he decided to leave in a hurry he wouldn't be able to go far but I don't know where he might have gone," Sarah said, rising to her feet. "I want to take another look at Bess," she said, and strode into the adjoining room.

Fargo sat back as thoughts raced through his mind. Bess was plainly intended to be another accident. He snorted at the word. Accidents planned and cleverly carried out. His thoughts leaped to Linda. She knew Bess was going to pay a visit to Sarah Trenchman.

The obvious conclusion virtually shouted out, yet he held back. It was too easy to make. Linda wasn't the only one who knew Bess wanted to find Sarah Trenchman. Bess had inquired all over town about Sarah. He couldn't point the finger at Linda, but he couldn't absolve her, either. She would remain that question mark for now.

Sarah Trenchman came from the other room to interrupt his thoughts. "No change. I'll keep watch on her," the woman said.

"What about getting a doctor?" Fargo suggested.

"The nearest Doc is way up in Deadwood. If he comes he can't do anything more for her than I'm doing now. There's not much you can do for a coma," Sarah Trenchman said.

Fargo frowned for a moment. "Can you keep her here, out of sight?" he asked.

"Sure," Sarah said.

"All right. I'll stop back soon as I can," Fargo said, and strode outside to the Ovaro. The torn piece of fabric burned inside his pocket as he rode back to the mine where he found Albert Darnville there with Linda and Roger.

"I expected you before this," Linda muttered to him, annoyance in her voice. He didn't answer. "Mister Darnville has made us an offer," she added.

"A generous offer," Darnville corrected. "A quarter million is most generous considering all the money I'll have to put into equipment."

"Of course, you'll give us time to talk it over," Roger said.

"Of course," Darnville said, smugly confident. "I'll stop back tomorrow." Roger walked outside to the surrey with him and Fargo saw the smoldering anger in Linda's blue eyes as she turned to him.

"What took you so long to get back?" she questioned.

"My horse had a loose shoe, left forefoot. I had to go to the smithy in town," Fargo said. "He has another coming loose I want to get taken care of right away."

"I expected you back earlier," Linda complained.

"Let's not play games, honey. You don't really need me yet, not till tonight," Fargo replied cooly.

Her eyes narrowed at him. "Don't be impertinent," she said sharply.

"Fire me," he shot back, grinning. He knew he was taking chances; he wasn't that sure of Linda yet. But she turned away without a reply. "Bess Darby stop back here today?" he asked.

"No," Linda said, not looking at him.

He kept his voice casual. "Anyone else know she was here asking about Sarah Trenchman?"

"Roger," Linda said. "He saw her leave yesterday and asked about her."

He kept his face expressionless as the answer blazed inside him. "You tell Roger everything?" he asked.

"Yes," she said. "I've no reason not to."

"Everything?" Fargo repeated, lifting one eyebrow.

"Almost everything," she corrected, and he laughed harshly as he turned away. "Where are you going?" Linda asked, frowning.

"To the smithy," he said. "I'll be back tonight."

"Make sure you are," Linda said demandingly as Fargo walked from the house. Linda's answers ran through his mind as he walked from the house. Roger knew Bess sought to find Sarah Trenchman. The fact made him feel better. It took some of the suspicion from Linda. Not all, but some. As he stepped from the house he found Roger waiting for him beside the Ovaro.

"Want to talk to you, Fargo," Roger said. "Free advice."

"Never turn down free advice." Fargo smiled. "Sometimes I even take it."

"Quit. Leave. Go your way," Roger said. "I'll even add a bonus to it."

"I've a job here," Fargo said.

"You're out of here soon as the mine is sold," Roger said.

"I'd say that'd be up to Linda," Fargo answered mildly.

"Don't get any ideas about Linda. She doesn't need a damn bodyguard and she'll send you on your way when she's through with you. I know my sister. She can't resist anything good-looking that wears pants and you're good-looking, I'll give you that."

"Thanks," Fargo said drily.

"But it's always short-lived with Linda, so you've no future with her. Take my word for it. So why don't you just leave now and I'll make it worth your while," Roger Ayler said.

"Linda's making it worth my while to stay," Fargo said. "But I'll think about it." He swung himself up onto the Ovaro and rode away. He rode toward town as dusk descended, but he turned west, climbed one of the hills, and rode back the way he had come.

He halted halfway up the hill beside a scraggly shadbush, where he had a clear view of the house, and settled down to wait. He was following a hunch. The night had descended when he saw the four riders appear below and rein up in front of the house. Roger Ayler came out and met with the men for a few minutes, then the four horsemen rode away. Fargo stayed on the hill as his eyes followed the four riders, a grim satisfaction settling over him. But satisfaction was not enough; he had to be certain. He started down the hill as he saw the four riders take the road to town. He followed, hanging back, and finally rode into Black Hills Junction where he found the four horses tethered together in front of the saloon. He dismounted and stepped into the saloon, locating the four men at the bar. His hands clenched as he took in the one at the end, wearing a dark-red shirt with black stripes.

He walked to the other end of the bar to get a better view of the man, his eyes moving down the man's shirt until he saw the torn place with the button missing. Ice formed inside him. One question had been answered even as others sprang up. Roger Ayler had engineered the made-to-order accident for Bess; had he arranged all the other accidents that had happened? If so, why? Ayler didn't want Bess pursuing her father's disappearance. What was he afraid she might discover? Another death? Was Sam Darby dead? The question that naturally followed shimmered in his mind. Was Linda involved? Or was Roger acting alone, a nervous keeper of his own secrets? As the questions whirled in his mind he returned his gaze to the four men at the bar. Maybe they could supply the answers, or at least some of them.

He drew back from the bar and sauntered from the saloon. Outside, he walked the Ovaro across the street into the deep shadows between two buildings and settled down to watch the customers come and go through the saloon's swinging doors. It was almost two hours and the night had grown long when the four men emerged. They mounted their horses and rode off together and Fargo cursed silently—he had hoped they would go their separate ways. Once again he followed them, leaving town riding south this time. Hanging back, he glimpsed them as they rode on along a road lined with bur oak. They showed no signs of splitting up and he decided there was no point in waiting any longer. He spurred the pinto into the oak, deep enough for the horse's hoof-beats not to be heard by the four men, made his way past them, rode on, and quickened the Ovaro's pace until he turned back to the road.

He halted in the trees at the edge of the road and drew the big Sharps from its saddle holster. Hidden in the trees, he raised the rifle to his shoulder as the four riders came into sight. He waited till they were closer and then called out. "Hold it right there," he said, and saw the four men rein to a halt. They peered into the trees where the black shadows cloaked him.

"You want money? Come get it," the one with the torn shirt growled.

"Don't want money," Fargo said. "Want some talk."

"Come out where we can see you," the man said.

Fargo smiled against the rifle stock. "You can talk from there," he said.

"We can shoot from here, too, mister," the torn-shirted one snapped.

"You can get killed from there, too," Fargo said.

He saw the four men exchange glances. He knew exactly what was going through their minds. They had more or less located him by the sound of his voice. If they all spray-fired at once there was a good chance they'd get him with at least one or two shots. But at least one of them would take a bullet, they realized, and they weren't the kind to be heroes, so they hestitated. "What do you want to talk about?" one called out.

"Arranging accidents," Fargo said. "Such as throwing a young woman off a cliff."

They weren't the hero kind, he was right about that, but he hadn't expected them to panic at his question. Yet that was exactly what they did, wheeling their horses and drawing guns. Fargo fired two shots from the big Sharps and two of the men toppled from their horses. The other two fired back, but wildly and Fargo ducked low as the bullets streaked harmlessly over his head. The two started to race away in different directions, and Fargo brought the rifle up again. He fired and one flew from his horse. Pushing the rifle into its saddle holster, Fargo spurred the pinto out of the trees and raced after the fourth man. He closed the distance quickly, the man fleeing in fear and panic. He was pushing his horse along the dark road, riding recklessly, and Fargo kept the Ovaro directly behind him as he drew the Colt from its holster.

The man glanced back in panic and Fargo saw it was the torn-shirted one and let the pinto close further. The man's horse was losing strength and speed, Fargo saw, unsure of its footing on the dark road, hind legs kicking out too wide. Suddenly the horse stumbled, forelegs going out from under it, and Fargo saw the animal go down, its rider tossed to one side. Fargo reined the pinto to a halt and leaped to the ground. The man was still on his hands and knees, shaking his head, as Fargo reached him in half a dozen long strides. Fargo held the barrel of the Colt to the man's temple as he pushed him flat on the ground with one foot against his back. He reached down and yanked the gun from the man's holster. "Just so you don't do anything else stupid," Fargo said, withdrew his foot, and stepped back. The man pushed himself up onto his elbows and turned.

Out of the corner of his eye, Fargo saw that the horse had regained its feet.

"Time for that little talk," Fargo said.

"Ayler told us to throw her off the cliff road," the man said.

"I know that. Why?" Fargo said.

"He never told us why. Honest, he never did," the man said.

"You arrange any other accidents for him?" Fargo questioned.

"A few," the man said.

"He give you any reason for those?"

"No. He just told us what he wanted done, that's all."

"Linda Ayler give you orders, too?" Fargo queried.

"No, just him," the man said.

"You met with him tonight. He give you any more orders?" Fargo pressed.

"No. It was pay-off time. He told us to come back in a few days," the man said.

"You won't be able to do that," Fargo said.

"You gonna kill me?" the man asked.

"I should, but I'm feeling kindly. I'll turn you over to the sheriff in Black Hills Junction," Fargo said as he backed to where the Ovaro waited. "Get up and get on your horse," he ordered, and the man pushed to his feet and started toward his mount. Fargo waited till the man had reached his horse before he started to pull himself onto the Ovaro. But the man's quick movement caught the corner of his eye. He dropped to one knee, an instinctive reaction, and saw the man whirl, the gun in his hand. Fargo's Colt barked before the man could get off a shot, the bullet slamming into the spot where his shirt was torn. He staggered backward before crumpling to the ground, the red stain already spreading across his chest. He'd had the second gun, a small, rimfire pocket pistol, inside his shirt. "Some people make it hard to feel kindly," Fargo muttered as he swung into the saddle and rode away.

He passed the other three silent forms on the road. They'd be found in the morning and it would be assumed they'd had a falling out. Even Roger Ayler, if he found out about them, would likely think the same. Fargo grunted, satisfied to have it that way for now. When he reached the mine and the main house there was no light on. It was late, he realized, and he went to the window of Linda's room. It was open a few inches at the bottom and he pulled it open enough to climb in. He walked softly to the bed and saw Linda sit up in the blue silk nightgown.

"Get out. You're fired," she said.

He didn't answer as he undid his gunbelt, took his shirt off, and then his boots. "What are you doing?" she frowned.

"Getting fired," he said as the top of the nightgown fell forward to reveal the lovely line of her breasts. He was excited and pulsating for her when he dropped the last piece of clothing to stand facing her. He saw her eyes fastened on him, her lips parting.

"Damn you, Fargo," she breathed. "Damn you," and she was reaching for him, moving across the bed, her hand closing around him. "Oh, Jesus, oh God," Linda gasped out, and he pulled the nightgown from her and pushed her back on the bed, joining her there. She held onto him, stroking, clutching, stroking again, and he pressed himself against her, his hand pushing through the little nap, finding her instant moisture. He came to her at once, sliding forward, and Linda cried out as she responded, lean legs rising at once to wrap around his hips. Remembering her raw wanting, he thrust deep and hard, throwing aside gentleness, patience, subtlety, and Linda screamed with pleasure. "Yes, yes, yes ... God, yes, harder, oh, Jesus, yes," she said, tossing out words in a breathless, gasping exhortation. When she finally clutched herself to him in a quivering crescendo, she made a deep, gutteral sound, ecstasy summoned up from her very core.

She lay limp and exhausted next to him when the moment dissolved and the world returned, opening her eyes only when he sat up. "Where are you going?" she murmured.

"Leaving. I was fired, remember?" Fargo said.

Her arms pulled him back down beside her. "You must have misunderstood me," she said.

"Sorry about that," he said, and she was asleep against him in moments. He smiled into the darkness of the room. Roger's harsh words about Linda had been intended as discouragement. He didn't understand that he'd furnished Fargo with a weapon, one that had just been confirmed. For a while, probably a short while, Linda was his, tied to him by her own carnality. He could think of worse ties, Fargo murmured to himself, as he closed his eyes in sleep.

6

He was dressed when she woke in the early dawn and she sat up to focus on him, resting on her elbows, large curved breasts peeking provocatively over the sheet. "Get back soon," she said. "Darnville's coming this afternoon."

"You and Roger decide to take his offer?" Fargo asked.

"We'll talk about it again this morning," Linda said. "I'll make the decision."

He paused at the window. "You ever think that maybe Roger might do things on his own?" he suggested noncommittally.

"Nothing important," Linda said, and Fargo nodded as he slipped from the window. The answer would seem to implicate her in everything Roger had done, but he was wondering more and more if Linda wasn't deluding herself. He hoped, for her sake, that was the case. Hurrying, he climbed onto the Ovaro and rode from the mine. He rode hard, turned at the pinnacle rock, and climbed High Cliff Road. When he reached Sarah Trenchman's house at the top, he saw the sorrel in the corral. The woman hurried from the house.

"He just showed up yesterday," she said of the horse. "Come in. Good news. Bess came out of it last night. She seems just fine." Fargo followed Sarah into the house and smelled the aroma of fresh-brewed coffee as Bess called from the other room.

"That you, Fargo?"

"Go in and see her while I finish making coffee," Sarah said, and Fargo stepped into the other room to see Bess sitting up in the bed, her shirt on and buttoned only in the center. But her brown hair, no longer pulled up atop her head, fell softly down to her shoulders, giving her a new attractiveness, more in keeping with the sensuousness of her mouth. She held both arms out to him and hugged him to her as he reached the bed, and he felt the full softness of her breasts.

"Thank you, Fargo. Sarah told me what you did," she said, pulling her arms away after a long moment. "I'm sorry I've been so—to use your word—bitchy. I guess I've been afraid of everything and everyone, Linda Ayler especially."

"I understand," he said.

"You still working for her?" Bess asked, no edge in her voice now.

"Still," he said.

"Sarah told me everything about the other men and how she feels my father's still alive. God, I hope she's right. You find out anything more?" Bess questioned.

"Roger Ayler's the one who tried to have you killed. He arranged some of the other accidents, too, maybe all of them," Fargo said.

"Roger Ayler?" Bess frowned, shifted, and he saw the top curve of one round, full breast push up over the edge of the shirt. "What about Linda?"

"I'm not sure she's involved. Right now I'd say she wasn't," Fargo said. He saw the skepticism come into Bess's face at once.

"She's gotten to you," Bess said. "I knew she would."

"Nobody's gotten to me. I haven't been able to tie Linda into anything. She thinks she's running the show, but she may not be," Fargo said.

"She's part of it, whatever it is. I know it," Bess insisted.

"How do you know it?"

"Inside. I know it inside," she said.

Fargo gave a half-grunt. He wouldn't accept her intuitions but he knew he couldn't ignore them, either. "It's all got to be connected to the mine somehow," Bess said.

"How, dammit?" Fargo snapped, more at himself than at her. "The gold has been assayed as excellent and they're about to sell the mine. I can't make any of this fit."

Bess's arms reached out to him again. "You will. I know you will," she said. "I'm glad she hasn't gotten to you and that you're keeping your distance until you find out more."

"I am, too," he said. Distance was a relative term, he told himself.

"You accused me of kissing only when I'm in a pout. This is to prove you wrong," Bess said, then her lips were on his, warm, soft, full of promise. The sensuous mouth was everything it appeared to be. Finally she drew back.

"That's not fair. I have to go," Fargo said.

"It's for you to take with you," Bess said with a touch of smugness as Sarah Trenchman entered the room with a wooden tray and three mugs of coffee.

"I want you to keep hiding out here," Fargo told Bess. "Roger Ayler thinks you're dead. I want him to keep thinking that. You'll be safe that way."

"She'll have to stay alone for the next two days.

I'm due at the Schneider place. Hilda is having her third baby," Sarah said.

"I'll be fine," Bess said.

"Anyone comes up looking for Sarah, you stay here in this back room," Fargo said, and Bess nodded. He drank his coffee, then left the two women together. He returned to the mine to find Chet Beamer's light Concord outside the main house. He dismounted and walked through the open door to find Beamer with Roger and Linda, an expansive smile on his face. Linda nodded to Fargo as he entered, but her attention stayed mainly on Chet Beamer.

"How did you know Albert Darnville made us an offer?" she asked Beamer.

"I had him watched. I know how he operates. He came here with Dodd to have your gold assayed. Then he left and came back the next day. When he left that day he was neither smiling nor angry. He'd made you an offer and you were going to think about it. Simple." Chet Beamer laughed. "And now you have mine," he said. The man exuded an arrogant confidence, Fargo noted.

The sound of wagon wheels came from outside and moments later Albert Darnville strode through the door, his brows lowered. "What are you doing here?" he barked at Beamer.

"Making an offer on the mine," Beamer said.

"They already have my offer," Darnville said.

"Now we have two," Linda put in.

"You have one. Mine is the only one you can consider. You contacted me to make an offer and I did. He wouldn't be here if I weren't." Darnville almost shouted. "I'm the one to whom you're morally and ethically bound."

"I'll leave you to iron this out," Beamer said to Roger and Linda. "You have my offer. I'll be in touch." He left with an easy swagger as everyone stared after him. Darnville's voice broke the ensuing silence.

"What did he offer you?" the man asked insistently.

"He said he'd double whatever you offered," Linda answered.

"That bastard. That's the way he works, throwing all his money around to freeze out everyone else. But he wouldn't have made you an offer if I hadn't. He's a moral parasite."

"That may be, but you really can't expect us to ignore an offer twice as good as yours. That wouldn't be right," Linda said almost soothingly.

"That's exactly what I expect you to do. That's the only ethical thing you can do," Darnville said, his face growing red with anger.

"We'll have to talk more about it," Linda said, and jumped as Darnville's fist came down on the table.

"Talk as much as you like, but you'd best come to the right conclusion," he thundered. "I came all the way out here at your invitation and I made you a proper offer. I expect you to honor your moral and ethical principles. I'm not letting Chet Beamer cheat me out of this deal the way he has others. Not again. I'll be back for your answer tomorrow," he said, spun on his heel, and strode from the house. Fargo peered from the doorway and saw him climb into his surrey, two of his men in the wagon.

"Didn't expect this much fireworks," Roger said. "But then, we didn't expect two offers."

Fargo's eyes found Linda's. "You're still in that catbird seat, I'd say," he commented.

"Yes, and I like it," Linda said. "But I'm more than a little frightened. Did you see how furious Darnville was? God knows what he'll do when we turn him down."

"'When?'" Fargo repeated questioningly.

"Of course. I'm not giving up an offer twice as good because he has some ideas of moral principles. Business is business," Linda said.

Fargo shrugged, not surprised and not able to completely fault her. She wasn't the first to set business aside from morality. Business is business, he echoed silently. The phrase was an old one and it implied that principles had little to do with making money. He'd never been completely comfortable with that. It seemed to say that greed and ambition were not held accountable to anything but themselves. But in all fairness he wondered if, were he faced with the same decision, would he be able to be so high-principled. He pushed aside his thoughts. He had other priorities.

"Guess this is your day," he said to Linda. "It seems Bess Darby has decided to go her way and look for her pa someplace else."

"What makes you say that?" Linda asked.

"Stopped in at the hotel in town. She hasn't been there for two days. I happened to meet Sarah Trenchman. She says Bess never showed up at her place," Fargo said. "I'd guess she got a new lead and took off after it." He flicked a casual glance at Roger. The man couldn't quite keep a note of satisfaction from his expression.

"Or she decided to take my advice and move on," Linda said. "But that doesn't affect the situation with Darnville. I'm still afraid of what he might do."

"Such as?" Fargo asked.

"Try to stop us from taking Beamer's offer, perhaps by force. The man's really beside himself,"

Linda said. Fargo peered at her and decided she really was fearful.

"What do you think?" he asked Roger.

"I don't know. It does make me somewhat nervous," he said.

"More than usual," Fargo said, and drew a quick glare from the man.

"I want you to stay here tonight, Fargo," Linda said.

"Whatever you say," Fargo agreed.

"You can use the room at the end of the hall," Roger said.

"I'm going to ride the area, have a look for myself. I'll be back by tonight," Fargo said, and hurried from the house. He'd wanted to visit Bess but a glance at the sky told him there wasn't time to do that and be back by nightfall. He rode to the low hill behind the house and surveyed the land, mostly open ground with a few clusters of shadbush and hawthorn. He was merely going through the motions. He didn't expect trouble from Darnville. The man didn't seem the type and there was no need for it yet. He still had time to try and convince Roger and Linda they were obligated to take his offer. Fargo uttered a snort at the thought and almost felt sorry for Albert Darnville. But Darnville wasn't his concern. Roger Ayler was his target.

The man had tried to have Bess killed, had succeeded with others, and he was about to sell a mine and walk away a rich man. Fargo swore in frustration. He still couldn't make any of it fit but he was certain it did fit, somehow, some way. Finding Sam Darby alive would provide the answers, he was sure. But there was no assurance of that, and time was becoming a factor. He swore again and made his way down to the house in time to see Roger riding down the road toward town. Linda greeted him at the door when he dismounted.

"Saw Roger heading for town," he commented.

"I sent him to do some errands," she said. "I'll show you the room." He followed her to the end of a corridor where she took him into a small but well-furnished guest room, a comfortable-looking bed against one wall.

"How about you visiting me tonight?" Fargo said.

"Roger will be awake most of the night. He's very nervous and he never sleeps when he's nervous," Linda said. "But he won't be back for at least an hour." Fargo turned to her and she was at him instantly, her fingers undoing buttons, pulling at his Levis, and then he was atop the bed and she was atop him, almost savagely plunging down on him, screaming with each downward thrust, a wildness on her that swept him along. Finally, gasping for breath, she lay beside him, thoroughly satiated. "God, you're all I think about," she murmured.

"More than selling a gold mine?" he asked wryly.

"That's different," she said.

"Roger doesn't think you'll be keeping me around long," Fargo remarked, and Linda pushed up on her elbows to peer at him.

"When did he say that?" she asked.

"The other day. He said you tired of a man pretty quickly."

"Roger should keep his damn mouth shut," Linda said, ice in her voice.

"I told you, maybe there's a lot about Roger you don't know," Fargo remarked, and realized he was hoping as well as probing.

"There's nothing about Roger I don't know," Linda said, and Fargo swore silently. It was not the answer he'd wanted. But once again, perhaps she simply

107

couldn't believe differently. He's still hold back judgment on her.

"Why would he say a thing like that?" Fargo asked.

"To get you to leave. He doesn't like outsiders around," Linda said.

"What's he afraid of?" Fargo questioned.

She hesitated a brief moment. "It's just the way he is," she said, an oblique answer that didn't satisfy him, but her arms came up, encircled his neck, and drew his head down to the lush curve of her breasts. "No more talk about Roger and his problems," she said and, pressing the tip of one breast into his mouth, effectively backed up her words.

Later, when she had gone to her room, he dressed and went outside into the night. Roger Ayler returned minutes later and Fargo watched him go into the house. He carried no grocery bags no packages of any kind and Fargo found himself wondering what errands Linda had sent him on. He swore softly. Little things continued to keep him from having complete faith in her. He went to the guest room and allowed himself the luxury of turning in early and sleeping late.

In the morning, he found a breakfast of rolls, bacon, and eggs waiting for him and Linda as sweet as a kitten as she served him. Roger sat by silently, and it was as if she was taunting him. When breakfast ended, Fargo went outside and rubbed down the Ovaro. He had just finished when Chet Beamer arrived in his light Concord. Fargo sauntered into the house after the man and turned to glance back as he heard another wagon approaching and saw Albert Darnville and two of his men in the surrey.

"Seems like a party coming up," Fargo said as he went into the house. Darnville stalked in alone mo-

108

ments later, his long face seeming even longer as he surveyed everyone with a sour stare.

"Gentlemen," Linda said pleasantly. "Roger and I have discussed everything. We feel it would be poor business, as well as ridiculous, not to accept the highest bidder. Therefore, Mister Beamer, we accept your offer."

"Wonderful." Chet Beamer smiled. "I'll be back tomorrow with a letter of agreement drawn up and a check drawn on my bank in Ohio." He ignored Darnville as he turned and strode from the house. Fargo watched Linda turn to Albert Darnville.

"I'm sorry," she said. "Someone has to lose."

"I'm not ready to concede that yet," Darnville said. "I've been going over my figures. Perhaps I can make another offer. I'll be back tomorrow, too, with a new offer and my own letter of agreement."

Fargo saw Linda exchange surprised glances with Roger. "Nothing's signed yet. We're still open," she said to Darnville.

"I expect you will be," Darnville said as he turned and walked from the house. Roger waited until he heard the surrey drawing away before he let out a half-shout of joy.

"This gets better and better. Beamer said he'd double Darnville's offer, so he'll get another chance, and we'll get more money," Roger said.

Linda's lips pursed in thought. "It's almost too good," she said.

"You're always so suspicious," Roger said.

"I don't like the wrong kind of surprises," Linda said.

"Neither do I," Fargo put in. "I'm going to scout around some. I'll be back later."

"Not too much later," Linda said as he walked from the house. He saddled the Ovaro and rode toward town, changed directions, and soon climbed High Cliff Road. Sarah Trenchman's house was still and silent when he rode to a halt and he entered and called out. The door to the back room opened at once and Bess rushed out, her arms going around him.

"You don't know how good it is to see you," she said. "It's hard staying cooped up, sneaking outside only to dart in again like a woodrat."

"I'm sure it is. Maybe it'll only be for another day," Fargo said.

"Why? Have you found out something more?" Bess asked.

"Not what you want to find out. Right now Roger Ayler is sitting pretty. Maybe the only way to get to him is to shake him up," Fargo said.

"You still think Linda's not part of it?" Bess questioned.

"I'm still not sure about her," he said truthfully.

"How can she not be involved?" Bess said.

"By being fooled. By thinking she's running things when she really isn't. By not being aware of what's happening under her nose. It goes that way sometimes. She wouldn't be the first," Fargo said.

Bess smiled, understanding in her face. "You're trying to be fair. That's commendable. Or it would be under other circumstances. I'm glad you're still keeping your distance," she said and her lips came to him, sweet softness, but he felt the compact energy of her body against him.

"I can't stay," he said.

"I know," she murmured.

"I'll be back tomorrow. I'll find more time," he said.

"Good. We can talk more then," she said, and he frowned slightly. It was the not the reply he'd expected. Or wanted.

"Meanwhile, you keep staying undercover," he said.

"I will," she said, clinging to him a moment longer before he left. He wondered about Bess Darby as he rode down High Cliff Road. There was still a properness to her. She could be the kind with a very real, very warm caring that stopped short of anything more, sincerity instead of sex outside of the marriage bed. That was a part of her, he was certain. But the sensuous mouth said there was another part of her, probably unexplored. He'd never had anything against exploring.

Bess Darby had her own prim intrigue, he decided, and closed off further thoughts of her as he reached the mine. He found only Roger in the living room of the house. "Linda's resting, in her room alone," Roger said. "Meditating, if you like. She gets that way sometimes, goes into a shell of her own. Thinking things out, she calls it."

"Doesn't seem there's much to think out. You just wait for Darnville's new offer and for Beamer to top it," Fargo said.

"That's the way I see it," Roger said.

Fargo paused for a moment and decided to lean on Roger Ayler a little more. "You remember anything more about why Sam Darby might have just up and left?" he asked.

Roger's glance was quick and nervously sharp. "No. Why are you still asking about him?"

"I heard that all the men you had working for you had fatal accidents. That sort of makes me curious." Fargo said.

"Coincidence," Roger snapped. "I wouldn't get too curious, Fargo."

"Bad habit of mine." Fargo smiled and wondered as he strode away if he only imagined Roger Ayler had added a new nervous tic to his face. Fargo went into the guest room and stretched out on the bed. He used the time to relax and try to make the pieces fit and finally realized there was no way he could do it, not until he had at least one key piece in hand, something that would tie together the elements that remained unconnected. He lay on the bed and watched the night descend, staying alone in the darkness until he finally rose and went outside. Linda was in the living room and had served up plates of cold mutton and heated carrot slices. She offered him a drink from a bottle of bourbon and he accepted. She toyed with her food, hardly spoke, and seemed thoroughly preoccupied.

"Want to tell me what's eating at you?" he asked. "Seems to me you ought to be happy as a lark."

"I'll be happy after tomorrow. I'm going to be alone tonight. I want more time to think. I don't want anything to interfere," Linda said coldly.

"What are you going to be thinking so hard about?" Fargo asked.

"That's my business, Fargo," she said, and he smiled agreeably. She had turned icily cold and he could feel her drawing into herself, away from him, from everyone. He didn't want that when he had so much to decide about her. He needed her to need him. He couldn't afford to lose the one hold he had on her. He watched her walk away without another word, her long, slender shape receding down the corridor to her room.

He glanced away to see Roger in the doorway. "You're out, Fargo. I told you as much," Roger smirked. "It was sooner than I expected."

"Enjoy yourself," Fargo said. "But don't count your chickens yet."

"I know Linda. When she turns herself off nobody

turns her on," Roger said and walked away, still smirking. Fargo went to the guest room and lay down in the darkness. He didn't know Linda as well as Roger did but he knew the messages of the flesh. Linda wasn't ready to turn herself off, not that much, though she was trying. She wasn't that satiated with him yet. He'd have picked up the signs when they were together. It might take a few days longer but it wasn't here yet. He'd wager on it. He let almost an hour go by before he rose, wearing only trousers, and went to Linda's room. He entered without knocking. She was in bed and she sat up at once, no robe on, no nightgown, either.

"Surpised?" she asked.

"No," he said.

"Damn you," she muttered and all but leaped at him as he went to her. The wild wanting was raging inside her and he met her every thirsting, urging demand until her final scream died away and she lay spent beside him. He slept beside her till early morning came, then he hurried back to the guest room.

He rested another hour before he washed and dressed and came out to the living room. Linda had fresh coffee and rolls ready. "You could become real domestic," he remarked.

"I get moods," she said.

"I know," he said, nodding, and she laughed and her arms were around his neck as Roger came into the room. Fargo enjoyed the astonishment on Roger's face as Linda drew away and poured coffee. After the breakfast dishes were cleared, Roger began to nervously pace the floor while Fargo relaxed in a chair. Linda sat alone, quiet, a tiny furrow on her forehead that grew deeper as the morning hours rolled into noon and Chet Beamer hadn't arrived.

"Where the hell is he?" Roger blurted. "He was so

damn anxious to sign. I expected him here first thing in the morning." Roger shot a glance at Linda but she remained quiet, her lips pursing and the furrow now part of her brow. Noon passed and Fargo found himself wondering, also. It was early afternoon when the wagon wheels sounded outside, and Roger almost ran to the door. "Shit, it's Darnville," he said. Fargo glanced at Linda. She remained motionless, wrapped in her own thoughts. She didn't change until Albert Darnville stepped into the room.

"Where's Beamer?" Darnville inquired.

"He hasn't come yet," Roger said.

Darnville let mild surprise cross his face. "Strange," he said. "But not entirely out of character."

"What's that mean?" Roger frowned.

"I'd rather not say yet. Let's wait a while longer," Darnville said, and sat down. Fargo's glance went to Linda, who hadn't said a word. Her cool blue eyes were studying Darnville. If Linda's silence surprised Darnville he didn't show it. He was no beginner at the bargaining game, Fargo decided, and a lot shrewder than he appeared to be. Only Roger seemed a poor match with his nervous pacing.

"You want a drink?" he asked Darnville at one point.

"No thanks," Darnville said pleasantly.

"Sit down, Roger," Linda said coldly as she sat back calmly. She was indeed a strange mixture, Fargo found himself thinking, retaining complete, icy control of herself except in bed. He sat back himself. He knew how to wait and watch, a lot better than any of the others. Darnville let another hour go by, the day well into mid-afternoon, when he rose.

"I'd say Mister Beamer isn't coming," he announced. "I'd say he backed out." He smiled, a chiding, smug smile.

"You seem awfully sure of that," Linda said, getting to her feet to face him.

"He's done this before. I told you it was not entirely out of character. He goes back and reexamines his figures. When he realizes he really can't afford all that the proposition will eventually take he simply disappears," Darnville said.

"I'd like to wait till tomorrow. Maybe something else stopped him from showing up today," Linda said.

Darnville shrugged pleasantly. "I've my letter of agreement with me but I can wait another day. I'm feeling generous, even though your willingness to deal with Beamer was inexcusable." He offered another more expansive smile as he left, and Linda waited until the sound of the surrey faded away before she turned to Fargo.

"Get into town. Find out what happened to Beamer," she said crisply.

"Good enough," Fargo replied with a nod and hurried from the room, curious himself at Chet Beamer's failure to appear. It was dusk when he reached Black Hills Junction and went to the hotel. He asked questions, refused to take answers without checking them out, rode through town peering into alleyways and behind buildings, paused at the town stable, and finally turned the Ovaro back along the road to the mine.

Roger was all but wringing his hands as Fargo entered the house, Linda waiting with cool patience. "He's not in town. Neither is his light Concord. I checked thoroughly. I'd say Darnville was right. He's backed down and left," Fargo told her.

Linda's cool-blue eyes were narrowed and she paid

no attention to Roger's curse. "We'll still wait till tomorrow," she said.

"We'll take Darnville's offer then," Roger put in with hollow bluster.

Linda turned to him. "We'll do what I decide to do," she said coldly, and Roger seemed to shrivel into himself before he hurried away.

"I'll come visit later," Fargo said to Linda when they were alone.

"No, not tonight. I've got too much to think out tonight," she said firmly.

"You sure?" he pressed.

"Very sure," she said, and he knew the other part of her had taken over, too completely to push aside for this night at least. He watched her stride away and he returned to his room, undressed, and lay awake for a while thinking of this latest surprising turn of events. He realized he oughtn't to be surprised any longer. He also realized one thing more before he fell asleep. Linda Ayler was still an enigma.

7

Fargo was up first when morning came, and he put the coffee pot on. Roger had some difficulty holding his cup steady when he appeared. Linda had no difficulty at all and Fargo noted the cool control was very much part of her. Darnville waited till past noon before arriving, and Fargo smiled to himself at the man's tactics.

"I take it Mister Beamer hasn't shown," Darnville said.

"No, it seems you were right. Fargo checked through town. He's nowhere to be seen," Linda said.

"Neither were the men he had with him," Fargo put in. "I checked everywhere, including the saloon. Didn't see a one of them. Didn't see any of your people, either."

"I let my men go. Didn't see any further need for them," Darnville said. "I can just take the next stage back myself when we're finished here."

"You brought your letter of agreement and a check, right?" Roger asked.

"Of course." Darnville smiled. "But there's been one little change. I've decided a hundred thousand is the best I can offer."

Fargo saw Roger's face drain of color and the man stammered, only little sounds coming from his lips.

He finally was able to form words. "You ... you can't do that," he said. "That's not fair."

Darnville shrugged. "It's completely fair, as fair as your willingness to take Beamer's offer."

"You bastard," Linda said, coldness in her voice.

"Come, now, that's not the way to talk to a prospective buyer. I might reduce my offer further," Darnville chided her.

"I might tell you where to shove your offer and start over again finding a new buyer," Linda said. Fargo saw the smugness leave Darnville's face. Her answer was plainly one he hadn't expected or wanted.

"Let's not be hasty. I'll go over my figures again. We can talk again tomorrow. Let's everyone take a little more time to think about this," Darnville said.

"Tomorrow," Linda said. Darnville gave a surprisingly gracious nod as he left. The surrey had only begun to roll away when Roger spun on Linda.

"Take his offer, whatever it is. Let's wrap this up and be done with it, dammit," he said.

"Beamer didn't back down," Linda said. "Darnville had him killed." Roger stared at her in shocked surprise and Fargo realized he was taken aback, too. It wasn't something he'd considered. "That's why he took until afternoon to show up," Linda said. "He knew Beamer wasn't going to show. He didn't need to get here first thing in the morning to bargain against Beamer."

"My God," Roger said, shocked awe in his voice, and Fargo found himself realizing the hard facts in Linda's conclusions.

"Poor Roger. He's surprised," Linda sniffed.

"You expected this?" Fargo frowned.

"I didn't but I'm prepared," Linda said. "Darnville was too furious to lose out again to Chet Beamer."

Fargo nodded and felt an admiration for the sharp coolness of her thinking.

"This really hasn't changed anything," Roger put in. "Tomorrow we take his offer, no matter what it is, and get out of here. I want to be finished with it."

"He won't really change his offer. When he thinks about it he'll realize we don't want to take all the time it'll take to search for a new buyer," Linda said.

"That's right. I don't want that," Roger said.

"And I won't let that weasel hold us up like this," Linda said.

"He's still offering a hundred thousand, dammit. Take it and be done with it," Roger said. "Before anything else goes wrong."

"What else can go wrong?" Fargo cut in.

"Nothing. Shut up, Roger," Linda said sharply.

"You think she's right about Darnville killing Beamer?" Roger asked Fargo.

"She just might be," Fargo said, and Roger turned away. Fargo felt the hairs on the back of his neck stiffening. A new tension crackled in the room. Roger's fear of something else going wrong hadn't been an empty alarm; Linda's sharp answer proved that. Fargo suddenly had the feeling that there was more than the sale of a mine at stake. Whatever it was somehow tied into the disappearance of Sam Darby and all the arranged accidents. He was certain of it now, based not on what had been said, but what hadn't.

He stared at Linda and Bess's question suddenly leaped out at him. *How could she not be involved?* Suddenly all the reasonable answers about Linda refused to suffice. He knew he needed time to think, to sort out what pieces he had, to step back and make new decisions on what to do.

"I'm going to keep a watch on Darnville, right through the day and into the night," Fargo said. "It might help."

Linda nodded, a pleased half-smile touching her lips. "Yes, it might indeed," she said. "But I want you here in the morning when he comes back."

"I'll be here," Fargo said, and hurried from the house with a last glance at Roger, who stared at the floor, his hands clenching and unclenching. Roger's nervousness had a new note of panic in it, and Fargo smiled as he rode from the house. Roger was the weak link and weak links are the first to crack. Fargo set aside further musings and concentrated on riding hard. He turned and sent the pinto up High Cliff Road at a canter. Bess came from the house as he reined to a halt and dismounted.

"Something's happened?" she said, searching his face.

"Yes, but I'm not sure exactly what yet," he said.

"That doesn't explain much." Bess frowned as she went into the house with him.

"I wish I could do better," he said and quickly told her everything that had taken place. She frowned again when he finished.

"One more," Bess said. "Maybe Darnville had Beamer killed and then maybe not. Nothing's for sure."

"Not yet. Let's go over what we know and what we don't know. Something might fall into place," Fargo said. "We know Roger Ayler tried to have you killed. We know he was behind all the other arranged accidents of the men who worked with your pa. We don't know why they were killed."

"We don't know if my father is alive. We don't know if he got away or if they caught him before he could run," Bess said.

"We don't know if Linda is involved," Fargo said.

"You don't know," Bess corrected.

"We don't know if there's a connection between their selling the mine and all those men being killed," Fargo said.

"I say there is," Bess snapped.

"What is it? I can't find how it fits. They could be two separate things," Fargo said.

"No, they tie in somehow, some way," Bess said. "This isn't getting us anywhere. There are too many things we don't know. The only thing we do know is that the Aylers are selling their mine and they'll walk away rich and we've no proof of anything to stop them."

"That brings us back to the start, why you came here. If we could find your pa alive we'd have all the answers we want," Fargo said. "Let's say he did get away in time. As Sarah said, he couldn't have gone far with a bad leg. Did he mention anyplace in one of his letters, someplace he might have gone to hide?"

"No. There weren't that many letters. He only mentioned Sarah a couple of times and we know he's not here. That's all there is around here except abandoned mine shafts," Bess said.

Fargo stared at her and felt his brow crease. "Jesus, that's it. Abandoned mine shafts. He could be hiding in one of the old shafts," Fargo said, excitement surging through him.

"How could he get food and water?" Bess frowned.

"Come out at night and catch food. Gopher, squirrel, fox, maybe even a young deer. He could make a snare for himself, store rainwater in a bucket. If he was in a deep shaft he could build a cooking fire and

121

nobody'd see the smoke, especially at night," Fargo said.

Bess blinked, the possibility pushing at her. "How could we find him? We'd have to check every old shaft."

"There aren't so many we couldn't do it," Fargo said.

"Wouldn't the Aylers have done that?" Bess asked.

"No, I don't think so," he said, frowning in thought. "If they missed getting him they probably figured he ran. They no doubt sent riders out to track him down, not figuring he'd hide under their noses."

"Then let's start looking," Bess said.

"Not till after tomorrow," Fargo said. "If they close a deal with Darnville they'll be less likely to watch what we're doing. They'll want to get ready to leave as soon as they can."

Bess leaned against him, her head resting on his chest. "At least now we have something to hope for," she said. Her arms lifted, came around his neck. "I'd be dead if it weren't for you. Not once but twice. I've been angry with you when I'd no right to be," she said. "I want to make that up to you." Her lips came up, and pressed his, the soft sweetness in them.

"You don't have to make up anything," he said.

"All right, no making up anything. What if I just want?"

"That'd be different," he said.

Her mouth found his again, sweetness taking on something more. "Consider it different," she said and her lips opened, stayed soft, but with a new insistence now. She moved backward into the other room, pulling him along with her as her lips stayed on his. Sinking down on the bed, she undid buttons as he took off his gunbelt and suddenly she had her blouse off and faced him, her compact body all roundness, breasts full and very round and high, almost as though they'd been molded into place with no real dip or cup to them. But they were very creamy with small, bright-red nipples on pale red circles.

He shed clothes as she wriggled out of her skirt and the rest of her was as compactly rounded as her torso, a fleshy little belly and a very full, deep black triangle, a short waist and legs that avoided being heavy by the firmness of youth, with full thighs and short, powerful calves. He sank down beside her, ran his hand across the round, full breasts, and she gave a tiny shudder that grew stronger as he gently circled one bright red nipple with his thumb. Tiny gasps came from her, little puffs of breath that grew in strength as his head came down and pressed into her breasts, his mouth finding one nipple and drawing it in.

"Oh, yes, oh, yes ... yes, yes," Bess cried out as her hands dug into his shoulders, suddenly sliding down to clasp around his waist and she rolled, carrying him with her, till she was pressing down onto him. "Oh, miGod, miGod," Bess said as she rubbed the deep, black triangle against him, sliding her round, compact torso up and down, up and down, and he felt the soft-wire nap against his erectness. She moved her body upward, pressed one round, full breast deep into his mouth, and moved it against his tongue, the soft fullness of it spilling over onto his cheeks. "MiGod, miGod, oh, yes, oh, I want, I want ..." Bess cried out and drew her breast back, pressed both round mounds over his face, and then he felt her wetness against his pulsating shaft and the fleshy thighs opened and she was sinking onto him and her scream of pleasure spiraled.

She was dark, wet softness around him, a pillowed

tunnel, engulfing, pressing, clinging, and she lifted her compact torso, almost pulled from him, then plunged down again, repeating the motion, finding a fervent rhythm and his hands closed around the full buttocks, helping, guiding, pushing. Bess's head shook, nodded up and down vigorously, then her lips were against his cheek. "Jesus, yes, yes, oh miGod yes," she muttered as her fervid pumping grew harder, faster, and suddenly she lifted her torso upward, strained her neck back, the full breasts just touching his mouth. She cried out, a long, song-like cry as her fleshy little belly slammed into his groin, held there, rose and slammed down hard again and he felt himself release with her, explosions of flesh to flesh, touch to touch, ecstacy to ecstasy and finally she dropped down atop him and he kept his hands closed around the soft, full rear.

She lay spent over him, but her thighs stayed tensed, holding him inside her as she made trembling little motions and sighing groans with each. Finally her fleshy thighs pulled straight and she fell from him, her arms pulling him with her, keeping his face pressed into her creamy breasts. "Aaaaaah, yes," she sighed. "So wonderful . . . so wonderful."

"And so long in between," he ventured and she nodded, the round breasts rubbing against his face.

"A long time, and never like this," Bess murmured. "Besides, I had one thing more to make up to you."

"What was that?"

"Telling you to keep your distance from Linda Ayler," she said. "I'm sure that wasn't easy. She's very attractive."

"It wasn't," he agreed, and brought his mouth down over one very red nipple. Bess groaned and her body responded at once, turning toward him, pressing against him, her hands pulling on him. But this time she was pulling him over her, pushing the dense soft-wire nap upward against him. The night came to wrap itself around their entwined forms and finally she sang her ecstacy into the darkness and he shared the shimmering moment with her. She curled herself against him soon after and he slept soundly, cradling her warm compact body against him until the new day finally came.

He was already dressed when she woke, swung instantly from the bed, and came to him, all full-fleshed and soft warmth. "When will you be back?" she asked.

"As soon as I can," he told her.

"Sarah Trenchman might come back today," Bess said.

"Good, but you don't have to stay shut in any longer. They won't have anyone out looking for you now," Fargo said and she held his hand against one round, full breasts before she stepped back.

"To help you hurry back," she said, and watched him ride away through the single curtained window. He rode slowly, his thoughts not on Bess but on Linda. He still held back on accepting Linda as the moving force behind everything that had happened, but the last twenty-four hours had made it hard to see Roger as acting alone on anything. It became even harder when Fargo reached the house and found Roger wrapped in nervous silence, his hands twisting, and Linda clothed in cool calm.

"Darnville stayed at the hotel all night," Fargo said.

"I expected that," Linda said and her eyes appraised Fargo. "You look rested for somebody's who's been up all night," she commented.

"I catnapped," Fargo said smoothly, and the sound of the surrey interrupted anything further.

Linda shot a quick glance at Roger, who rose at once and left the room. She caught Fargo's quizzical frown. "We agreed last night that I'd handle this alone," Linda said.

"That my cue to leave, too?" Fargo asked.

"No, you stand by. You'll add strength, not weakness," Linda said, and turned as Albert Darnville strode into the room.

"Good morning, Linda," he smiled. "I'm sure we can conclude our business this morning."

"I'm sure of it," Linda said.

"I've gone over my figures again. I'm not offering anything more than I did yesterday," Darnville said, hardness coming into his voice.

"I think you will," Linda said calmly, reaching into a pocket inside her skirt. She brought out a square piece of paper and pushed it at Darnville. "I suggest you read this," she said. Albert Darnville opened the folded square of paper and stared down at it. Fargo watched the frown cross the man's face. "Why don't you read it aloud for us?" Linda said almost sweetly.

Darnville's voice came from him as a deep, growling sound. "Albert Darnville ordered us to kill Mister Beamer. Zach and me did it but Darnville paid us special to do it. Hank Drewson." Darnville's eyes were narrowed as Linda took the piece of paper from his hands.

"You see, I expected you'd try something like that and I was ready. You paid off your men and sent them on their way. Only I saw to it that Hank Drewson didn't get far," Linda said.

"You bitch," Darnville rumbled. "You can't use this."

"Of course I can," Linda said.

126

"Hank Drewson won't back it up. It'd be putting his own neck in a noose," Darnville said.

"No it wouldn't. He'll be safe across the border in Canada. He can back up his confession from there," Linda said.

"They'll insist he come to court to testify," Darnville countered.

"Maybe, and then maybe not. They don't always. You want to take that chance? You want to risk your neck on that? I'd say when this note comes out you won't be worth much in your precious financial circles," Linda said.

Fargo realized that he shared the surprise that he saw in Albert Darnville's face. The man had been taken completely aback and only his anger held him together. His lips twitched and Fargo watched emotions race across Darnville's face. Linda looked on with icy poise. She was absolutely remarkable, he found himself thinking, a split personality, a slave to erotic drives and an ice princess. Darnville's voice cut into his thoughts as the man glowered at Linda.

"My first offer, quarter of a million," Darnville growled.

"Beamer doubled that. Match it," Linda said.

"I can't. It's as simple as that. I'll need money to develop the mine. I can't go any higher, no matter what kind of note you have," Darnville said.

Fargo's eyes were on Linda and he saw her lips purse in thought. "All right," she said after a long moment. "You draw up a bill of sale?"

Darnville nodded, took the agreement from his pocket, and handed it to her. She read it quickly and put it on the table. "Change the numbers," she said, stepped to a small desk against the wall, and brought Darnville a quill pen and an inkstand. She watched as he crossed out numbers and put in the corrected ones. Fargo searched her face. He found no softening, no hint of happiness, only cold triumph. "Roger, get in here," Linda called out as Darnville finished. "We've a bill of sale to sign." Roger appeared almost instantly and with a nervous nod to Darnville, signed the agreement. "You next," Linda told Darnville. "I'll sign last."

"What about Drewson's letter?" Darnville asked as he signed.

"You'll get it as soon as we have the money. We'll send it to you," Linda said.

"You have my check. It's perfectly good," Darnville snapped.

"Soon as we cash the check the letter's yours. You have the bill of sale now. You own the mine. You have what you want. I just want to be sure we have what we want. It's called prudence," Linda said.

"The bank in town has a certified letter from my bank in Ohio guaranteeing the funds to cover my check," Darnville said. "Present the check and they'll give you the money, or their check for it."

"Good. Soon as I do that I'll leave Drewson's letter for you at the hotel," Linda said.

Darnville fastened a slightly chiding glance on her. "You've got to learn to trust people, young woman," he said.

"You, too," Linda returned. "Soon as I visit the bank you get the letter."

"It seems I've little choice in the matter," Darnville said, shrugging. "Then I think our transaction is all but finished. I have the mine and that's what I came to get. You drive a hard bargain, Miss Ayler."

"You did some hard driving yourself. I think Chet Beamer would agree with that," Linda remarked. Darnville's eyes narrowed at her, then he turned and strode from the house. Linda didn't move until she heard the surrey rolling away. Then she turned to Roger, who slumped into a chair. Fargo noticed he was perspiring. "It's over. I told you it'd go our way," Linda tossed at him, almost with a sneer. "You're so damn weak-kneed, Roger."

"Go to town. Finish it," Roger said, pleading in his voice.

"You need a drink, Roger. Go get one for yourself," Linda said.

"Jesus, yes," Roger muttered as he rose and hurried from the room. Fargo found himself staring at Linda with a kind of awe that refused to embrace admiration.

"How and when did you manage to get hold of Drewson and get that letter out of him?" he questioned. "That's one thing I can't figure."

Linda turned a smug smile on him. "I didn't get hold of Drewson. I wrote the letter and signed his name to it," she said.

Fargo felt the wave of astonishment sweep over him and knew he stared open-mouthed at her. "It was all a damn bluff?" he said.

"Not really. More of a calculated guess. As soon as I was convinced that Darnville had Beamer killed I knew I had to be ready with some countermove. When he said he'd paid off his men and sent them on their way I knew I was right. Remember the other night when I sent Roger to town on some errands?"

"Yes, and I remember he didn't come back with anything." Fargo nodded.

"You noticed that, did you?" Linda smiled. "But I'm not surprised. You don't miss much. What he brought back were the names of Darnville's men. All I had to do then was write the letter and have it ready. It all worked out exactly as I expected it would, though I did want Darnville to match Beamer's offer. But then, we can't be greedy, can we?" She smiled again, savoring the moment privately.

Fargo stared at Linda as the thoughts whirled through his mind. He was awed by the sheer audacity of what she had done but there was more than just that. He stood in awe of the realization that swept through him. Two indisputable truths rose up above all else, above Linda's cleverness, above her boldness, above her icy determination. The first was that Albert Darnville had indeed ordered Chet Beamer killed. He hadn't known that Linda's letter was a pure fake, a total bluff. But he'd conceded to the truth of what she had written. He'd admitted his guilt based on that. The truth had come out though it was wrapped in deceit, and Fargo grunted at the irony of that.

The second truth shouted at him just as clearly. Linda had planned quickly when she had to do so. She had been in total control as Roger had almost come apart with fear. That was no sudden role reversal. It had always been that way. Roger had never done anything on his own. Everything had always been planned and directed by Linda. Roger may have hired the men to arrange all the strange accidents that had taken place, but never on his own. He'd been working under orders—Linda's orders. There was still a connection that refused to tie in, though, a piece that refused to fit. Only yesterday Roger had urged Linda to accept any offer *before something else went wrong*. Roger's words danced in front of Fargo.

What else could go wrong? Fargo pondered the question and decided it had to connect with that piece that still refused to fit. Linda's voice interrupted his thoughts. "I'm going to the bank in town. I want you with me, just in case," she said. "Wait outside while I get my horse." Fargo nodded and stepped out to stand beside the Ovaro. Linda's preemptory tone was not completely sudden, but it had just taken on a new dimension and he wondered how soon she'd be sending him on his way. It might be fun to see if he still had that one hold over her. It had really been the only card he'd ever had. Maybe he could play it one last time. He climbed onto the Ovaro as Linda came out astride a tan gelding, and he rode beside her toward town.

"I'd say you ought to be pretty damn pleased with yourself," he commented.

"Yes, I agree." She laughed.

"Looks as though you won't be needing a bodyguard anymore," he said.

"I guess not," she said. "Let's talk about that tonight, after I finish with the bank. We know Albert Darnville can be very unpleasant under that proper businessman's façade."

"Yes, we do know that, don't we?" Fargo agreed, and rode the rest of the way in silence. He waited discreetly to one side at the bank as Linda closeted herself with the bank president. When she came out he saw the final triumph in her eyes.

"Finished. I've the bank check," she said to him as they rode from the bank in the gathering dusk. She halted before the hotel and handed Fargo a small envelope. "Drewson's letter. Leave it at the desk for Darnville," she said. He obeyed and returned to the pinto. "A bargain's a bargain. One has to keep one's word," she said as they rode off. He caught the mocking tone inside the words and was surprised. Self-mockery didn't fit Linda. She was laughing at something else. It was dark when they reached the house and found Roger sprawled over the table. The man raised his head as Linda came in. Roger had

had more than one drink. "Take him to his room and leave him there," Linda said.

"How about please?" Fargo asked. "I'm a bodyguard, not a nurse."

Linda's eyes narrowed for a moment, but a half-smile accompanied her concession. "Sorry. I'm used to giving orders. Please," she said, and watched him lift Roger over his shoulder and carry the man down the hall. He dropped Roger on the bed in his room and closed the door. Linda had brought a bourbon bottle and some cold beef out, and he sat down across from her. "What if I wanted you to stay on with me? We spoke about that," she said.

"I'd have to think about it," he said, downing the bourbon. "I'd want to be sure."

"Of what?" she asked.

"Of how much you needed me."

"You surprise me," Linda said. "I thought you'd be sure of that."

He half-shrugged and allowed a sheepishness in his smile. He wanted her to feel more in control than usual. "Guess I'm not," he said, rose to his feet, and came to stand very close to her, his crotch almost touching her face. She finished her drink, a long, slow sip.

"Don't you think you ought to sit down?" Linda murmured, not looking at him.

He moved even closer. "No," he said, took her face and turned it, pressing it against him.

"Oh, Jesus . . . damn you, Fargo," Linda murmured into his trousers, and then he was lifting her, carrying her to her room. He tossed her onto the bed and began to shed clothes at once. It almost became a race as Linda flung off blouse and skirt and was clutching at him as he came to her. He was ready and throbbing at once, the raw charged moment an arousal of itself. She took him in her hands, pressed, caressed, brought her lips to him. The room vibrated with the sound of her screams as, more than ever before, she abandoned herself to the driving, erotic needs inside her body. Even as he met her demands, brought her to that final pitch of fervor, he knew it was different this time for him. It was the final game, all the stakes on the bed, and when she climaxed with total pleasure he lay half-over her, drawing the last moment of ecstacy from the moment.

Then, as always, she became sweet and soft, thoroughly satisfied. He knew now that this was the only moment Linda ever became vulnerable, and he lay with her, nuzzling, letting his hands and lips stroke her long, lean body while she murmured contentedly. "When will you be leaving?" he asked casually into her breast.

"Soon enough. There's no rush," she said.

"Too bad about Bess Darby?" he said with continuing casualness.

"What about Bess Darby?" Linda asked.

"Her not being able to find out what happened to her pa," he said.

"Yes, too bad," Linda sighed.

"And the funny accidents that happened to all the other men who worked with him," Fargo said. He listened to the moment of silence and then felt Linda rise on one elbow. He drew his face from her breast. A cold caution had slid into her eyes and he swore at himself.

"What funny accidents?" she asked.

"Just things I heard about. Forget it," he said, and offered a smile. It didn't soften her eyes, he saw.

"You forget it. Maybe you shouldn't listen to idle talk. Accidents are accidents," Linda said.

"Sure," Fargo agreed soothingly. But he knew he

had failed. She hadn't let anything slip in her mood of vulnerability. Perhaps he had expected too much of that moment. Perhaps there was never any real vulnerability to Linda. Perhaps there was only fire and ice and neither gave up secrets. But he had to try again and he brought his lips down to her breasts. He felt her hand push him away, almost a slap.

"I think you should leave now," she said.

"What's the matter?" he asked innocently.

"I want to decide about things alone," Linda said, and he swore silently again.

"I thought you just did that," he said, and cupped his hand around one breast.

"We'll talk in the morning. Please leave," she said coldly.

He shrugged and dressed, slowly and deliberately, aware that she watched him, and he saw the struggle in her eyes. But, as he had learned, Linda was two people. Perhaps his attempt never had a chance. The wild abandonment of her lovemaking, more than it had ever been before, was perhaps her way of writing an end to her need of him. He paused at the door and looked back at her. She lay unmoving on the bed, her naked beauty glacially lovely, her face expressionless. He closed the door and hurried away.

8

In a morning made of bright sun, Bess rode beside Fargo down High Cliff Road. He had decided they could not search by night; the old mine shafts were dangerous enough even by day. Bess had insisted on coming with him, and she had made sense. "If he's still hiding in one of the deep shafts he certainly won't come out for you calling him," she had said. "But he will if he hears my voice."

Fargo had agreed, and boldness became the mark of the morning. "What if we don't find him?" Bess asked as they reached the bottom of the cliff road. "They just leave with all that money and we never know what happened."

Fargo grimaced, the assessment all too accurate. "We have a few days," he said. "I don't think they'll be leaving before that."

"What if we don't find my father? What if we can't make that missing connection?" Bess asked. "They just go their way rich and happy. I hate the thought of that."

"I'm not much for that, either. Let's wait and see before we wrestle with that," Fargo said as they reached the house, rode past it, and up the first hill. Reaching the boarded entrance to the mine, Fargo pulled down one weathered board to give them enough room to enter. But not before he surveyed the ground around the entrance with his trailsman's eye.

"No footprints," Bess said.

"No, but that doesn't mean anything. Didn't expect to find any," Fargo said.

"Why not?"

"He'd have been smart enough to erase them," Fargo said.

"Then what were you looking to see?" Bess frowned.

"Signs of tracks being wiped away. That's where most people who wipe away tracks make their mistake. They don't know how to cover up their cover-up. That takes experience," Fargo told her and she listened with her eyes widened. "Let's take a look inside," he said, and led the way through the opening he'd created.

The damp, musty odor assailed his nostrils at once and he drew in a deep breath in an attempt to take in something else, but there was nothing. Bess followed him down the long, sloping shaft. The shoring on the walls held his attention for a few moments, then he went on until the light grew dim. The shaft continued on downward and he stepped aside to let Bess stand in front of him. "Daddy? You down there anyplace?" Bess called out. "It's me, Bess."

They listened but the only sound was the echo of her voice rising up from the depth of the shaft. She called again, then again, waited longer, and finally Fargo touched her elbow. "Let's go," he said gently. "This isn't it." She followed him from the abandoned mine and he led the horses diagonally across the hill to where another boarded opening beckoned. There were enough gaps between the boards to enter and, after scanning the ground at the entrance, he went inside with Bess close on his heels. The dank, musty odor was the same, but this shaft was larger. It ended in a steep drop, though a wooden ladder still remained in place. Fargo climbed down the ladder and Bess followed, and they halted at another long shaft filled with darkness. Bess called out, the same plea, calling her father by name this time. She called again, repeated her own name, and only the echo answered from the bottom of the shaft.

"Let's go," Fargo said, and let her climb the ladder first. He paused to examine the shoring again on the way out. Clambering out behind Bess, he bumped into her as she stopped in her tracks and he looked past her to see Linda and Roger, both on horseback.

"What's going on here? What is this?" Roger queried with a frown. Fargo glanced at Linda and saw her eyes were on Bess.

"What are you doing here?" Linda snapped at Bess.

"I came back to look some more for my father," Bess said and Fargo glanced at Roger. The man's eyes were staring at Bess, disbelieve in his face.

"Back from where?" Roger muttered.

"From almost dead," Bess said. Fargo was proud of her. She was playing it just right, and he saw the uncertainty in Roger's face. "Fargo agreed to help me," Bess added.

Linda's eyes went to Fargo. "I thought you were working for me," Linda said.

"Not anymore. Did some deciding myself last night. I quit," he said.

Linda's cool blue eyes were narrowed as they studied him. "I'm wondering if you ever really worked for me," she said.

"A good question." Fargo smiled.

"You bastard. I underestimated you," she said.

"Always a mistake."

"You were using me."

"And you were using me," Fargo said.

Roger's voice cut in. "You're finished here. Get moving," he said.

"We're not near finished. We've a lot of looking to do," Fargo said.

"Get off. This is private property," Linda snapped.

"I know, but not yours," Fargo said, and saw her eyes harden. "You've no right chasing us off. This belongs to a man named Albert Darnville. He's the only one that can chase us off."

"Dammit, I don't care about that," Roger said.

"Shut up, Roger," Linda said. "He's right, of course. We wouldn't do anything illegal." She wheeled her horse and rode away, Roger following with a last, frowning glance back at Bess.

"Let's go on. We can search one more before the daylight runs out," Fargo said to Bess.

"They going to leave us alone?" Bess asked.

"Wouldn't bank on that. I'd guess they'll be watching us the way a fox watches a henhouse, until we come up with your pa or leave empty-handed," Fargo said, and led the way to the next abandoned mine entrance. Inside, it was little different than the first two and again he examined the wooden beams that shored up the walls of the shaft. They were much like those in the other shafts. Again, there was no answer to Bess as she called out.

It was dusk when they emerged and he led the way down from the hills. "What if Sarah's come back?" Bess asked as they climbed High Cliff Road.

"I'll sleep outside in my bedroll," he said.

"What if she hasn't?" Bess asked, slyness in her voice.

"Dumb question," he said.

138

"Yes," she agreed, and smiled when they reached the house and found Sarah hadn't returned.

Later, when she lay with him, satisfied and exhausted, asleep in his arms, he wondered if there was a way to do what had to be done without risking her neck. He had seen the icy fury in Linda's eyes and he knew she would stop at nothing. In a strange, reverse way, Bess would be better off if they didn't find her father. He closed his eyes without answers and when morning came he was in the hills again, Bess at his side.

Linda and Roger were watching, he knew, probably from the house below, perhaps behind one of the hills. But watching, waiting. That was certain. He felt it inside himself. The first of the mines they entered was larger than the others but brought no more results that the others had. By the end of the day they had explored three more of the old mine shafts with no results and they finished with but one hillside left to search. Sarah Trenchman had returned, they found when they climbed back atop the distant hill, and one glance at Bess led the woman to suggest that Fargo share the back room. Bess threw her a grateful smile, and when they had finished telling Sarah all that had happened, he retired to the room and Bess followed in moments.

"Sarah said that if we find my father we should bring him to her," Bess told him as she lay beside him.

"This might be the best place," Fargo agreed.

"Might be?" Bess questioned.

"I don't want to risk anybody else's neck if I don't have to," he said.

"Of course. I didn't think about that," Bess said. Her lips found his and she made love to him with her compact body finding a new, slower warmth that was unexpected and thoroughly delightful.

When the new day came they rode to the last hill together. Fargo scanned the ground before the first of the old shafts as he had done with all the others, and put a hand on Bess's arm as she started to enter the mine.

"Maybe we've got something," he said, feeling the excitement spiral through him.

"I don't see anything." Bess frowned as she watched him kneel and examine the ground. "It's all smooth."

"Too smooth," he said. "The wind hasn't had time to ruffle it. I'd say it was smoothed late last night." Bess's eyes grew wide and he stepped into the old mine with her. He saw a long, deep shaft, narrower than some of the others had been, and they walked softly down the tunneled walls, stopping only when the light began to fade away. Bess glanced at him and he nodded.

"Daddy?" she called. "It's me. Are you down there anywhere? Daddy? Can you hear me? I've come looking for you." She waited, listened, and Fargo strained his ears and nodded to her again. "It's all right, Daddy. It's me, Bess," she called again. The sound came from deep in the shaft, faint at first, then stronger, and Bess gasped and raised her voice in excitement as she called once again. The sound filtered up to where Fargo stood beside her, became the shuffling of footsteps, and the figure began to emerge from the darkness of the shaft, pickax in hand. Then Bess was flying down the corridor, crying out tiny excited sounds of joy and relief.

Fargo saw her rush into the man's arms, pulling him to her with an embrace, then finally coming forward with Sam Darby. Fargo saw a man hardly taller than Bess, with a slight limp in his right leg. A grizzled graying beard and a lined face with dark, deep brown eyes gazed at him. "This is my friend, Fargo," Bess said. "He's been helping me look for you."

Sam Darby nodded and Fargo saw that the man had kept himself remarkably neat and clean. "How'd you figure I was here?" Sam Darby asked.

"Fargo put it together," Bess answered. "We were hoping you'd gotten away."

"I did, just in time. They had those four hands of theirs coming to get me. This old shaft was the only place I could get to, and then I found out I was trapped here," the man said.

"Did you try to get out?" Bess asked.

"A number of nights," her father answered. "But they had those four bastards patrolling the hills and with this bad leg I moved too slow. By day it was out of the question. In time they probably figured I'd gotten away. I'm sure they put up a good search."

"You're talking about the Aylers, of course," Fargo said.

"That's right," Sam Darby said, nodding. "I decided the only thing I could do was to stay holed up here until they sold the mine. It took a lot longer than I expected it would. I guess they finally did. That's why you got to search for me."

"They sold it but they're still here," Fargo said, and saw a moment of fright come into the man's eyes. "We came searching because we decided we couldn't wait any longer. They're about to clear out with a lot of money."

Sam Darby gave a wry snort. "They did it, the bastards," he said.

"What's the connection, Sam? How does it all fit—you expecting them to sell the mine and hiding out here?" Fargo asked. "We know about all those arranged accidents."

Sam Darby set the pickax down and lowered himself onto a mound of earth. "They hired us all to do a special job for them, a special mining job, they told us. They gave us real good pay and the promise of another big bonus when we finished. All we had to do was do our jobs, no questions asked."

"Which was what?" Fargo put in.

"Make a gold mine they could sell," Sam said, and Fargo felt his brows lift. "You see, all these other shafts were really no good. They all had a few surface veins but nothing else. That's why the Aylers finally shut them down. But they all had a little gold, a few veins, not enough to mean anything big."

"They had you take all those veins, all the dirt and the gold in it, and put it into that one mine," Fargo said.

"That's right. It took a lot of work, over a year, and lots of times we worked at night. But we did it, making new deposits out of old ones, building new walls with gold veins deep enough to fool most anyone."

"That accounts for the shoring," Fargo said, and Sam Darby frowned.

"The shoring?" he echoed.

"Yes. I kept noticing new shoring built alongside old shoring. The old shoring was there but you had to put up new planking when you reconstructed the mine shaft walls," Fargo said.

Sam Darby grinned. "That's right. That's just what we did. You don't miss anything, do you, Fargo," the man said admiringly. "Most folks wouldn't notice that at all."

"I make a living noticing things," Fargo said.

"So the Aylers sold Darnville a phony mine," Bess said.

"With real gold in surface veins to pass any assayer's test," Fargo said. "And deep enough to satisfy a quick inspection."

"Of course, they never told us that was what they were doing, but it didn't take a hell of a lot of brains to figure they were up to something," Sam Darby said. "Hell, we didn't really care. They paid us real well. All they had to do was give us the bonus when the job was finished and we'd have gone on our way. But they decided they couldn't take the chance that somebody might talk."

"So all the fatal accidents began to happen," Fargo said, and the man nodded.

"I believed that's what they were, at first. We all did. But then I began to get suspicious. Maybe 'afraid's a better word. After John Masters had his accident I knew I was next on the list. I was the last one of us left. That's when I decided to clear out. But I wasn't fast enough. They came for me that night and I had to run for it."

"So suddenly you left your Bible," Bess said. "When I found it I knew you hadn't just walked away as the Aylers said."

Sam Darby hugged his daughter to him. "Thank God for a new use for the Good Book," he said, then turned to Fargo. "What now, young feller?" he asked.

"We take you out of here and then I bring in the Aylers and Albert Darnville," Fargo said. "You have anything you want to bring out with you?"

"A few things in my backpack. I'll get it," Darby said, and limped down the tunneled corridor as Bess held tight to Fargo.

"We did it. You did it," she said.

"We. You came looking. That's what started it," he said, and her father returned, the pack slung over his back. He walked alongside Bess as Fargo led the way back to the entrance of the shaft. Fargo paused at the planking across the mouth of the mine and drew his Colt, bending over as he crawled from the entranceway. "Come on out, but only a step or two," he said, and reached in to help Sam Darby crawl out. Sam had just emerged to stand beside Fargo when the shots rang out, three explosions of long-distance rifle fire. Fargo practically threw Sam Darby back into the mine entrance and hit the ground to crawl under the planking himself as another shot slammed into the wood.

"My God," Bess breathed.

"Half expected that," Fargo said. "But there was only one way to find out." He huddled behind the wooden planking with Bess and her father, peering down the hillside. But there were no more shots.

"What do we do now? They can keep us pinned down in here," Bess said.

"We go back inside and wait," Fargo said.

"For what? For them to try and rush us?" Bess asked.

"No, they won't do that. They'll just keep watching and waiting. But they won't be able to see come night," Fargo said. "We'll get out of here then." He cast a glance out of the old mine to the sky. "I'd guess we've a few hours wait. Let's go back inside, away from the entrance, in case they try shooting from higher on the hill."

He led the way into the shaft and lowered himself against one of the dirt walls. Bess sat down across from him with her father. "They'd have gotten clean away with all of it if you hadn't come looking for me," Sam Darby said. "I'd have come out in time but nobody would've believed me all by myself."

"They'll believe you now, with what we can add to it," Fargo said.

"How's Sarah?" Bess's father asked.

"Well. She's done a lot of worrying over you. She'll be glad to see you," Bess told him. They were still idly talking, strangely confident, when Fargo heard the sound of racing hoofbeats nearing the entranceway and leaped to his feet. He was staring up the shaft when the explosions rocked the walls first one, then two more. He saw Bess and Sam fling themselves to the ground as pieces of wood shoring and rock cascaded all around them.

"Dynamite," Fargo bit out. "Goddamnit, dynamite." He spit dirt from his mouth as silence descended and he pushed to his feet to see that the mouth of the mine was no longer there. Instead, a small mountain of dirt, rock and wooden planks blocked the entranceway. He saw Sam and Bess get to their feet, pieces of rock and mounds of dirt making the shaft a narrow place now.

"Damn their stinkin' hides," Sam Darby said. "They've sealed us in here." Fargo walked to the mountain of rock blocking the mouth of the mine and saw where the ceiling of the shaft had collapsed. The dust that filled the air was in his mouth and he blew it out but the dank, damp odor pushed itself into his nostrils. He couldn't find even a crack of light through the mountain of rock and dirt. He turned to Sam Darby.

"You're a miner. How long do we have before we use up the air in here?" Fargo asked.

Sam Darby screwed his lined face up for a moment. "No fresh air coming in and three of us breathing, I'd guess maybe till morning. Air gets used up pretty fast," he said.

"You've a pickax. How long would it take us to hack our way through this?" Fargo pressed.

"There's some heavy rock in there. I don't know that we could get through it. But it'd take us a couple of days, at least," the man said. "The more energy we spend the deeper we'll breathe and the faster we'll use up the air."

"We have any choice?" Fargo said.

Sam Darby drew a deep sigh. "We can sit quiet and breathe soft. Sometimes a pile of new slide like this will shift by itself and give us some air."

"If it doesn't?" Fargo questioned. Sam Darby shrugged helplessly.

"I don't like it," Fargo said. "I'm not going to sit around and wait to suffocate. I'd rather suffocate trying to get out."

"I'd rather that, too," Bess said.

"Your choice. I'm sort of on borrowed time anyway," Sam said.

"We'll work in shifts," Fargo said, lifting the pickax.

"Wait. The light's already going. I've a few candles I used deep down in the shaft. I'll bring them up, if I can get back down there now," Sam said and hurried off, clambering over newly fallen rock and mounds of dirt. Fargo felt Bess's hand take his.

"I'm sorry. I should never have gotten you involved," she said.

"Things happen," he told her and held her to him. He heard Sam stumbling his way back and the man appeared with two lighted candles inside the glass shells of old kerosene lamps. "Found them here when I arrived. We often use candles to tell us the

146

air flow," Sam said and sat the two holders on opposite sides where they lighted the mound of earth.

"I'll start," Fargo said, lifting the pickax and plunging it into the dirt. He struck rock instantly and felt the shudder travel through the pickax and up into his arms.

"No, not there," Sam said, and Fargo saw the man's eyes peer upward to the top of the earthern mound. "Up there, where it's against the roof of the tunnel. That's where it stopped coming down. The dirt will be loosest up there. All we need is enough room to crawl over the top and down the other side."

"Always listen to experience," Fargo said as he climbed the slanting mound to the very top. He plunged the pickax in and immediately felt the looseness of the soil. He began to work, plunging the ax in and pulling out dirt and small rocks. But it was an awkward position in which to swing the tool and after half an hour he felt the muscles of his legs cramping even more than his arms and shoulders. When he finally slid from the earthen mound to rest he realized how pitifully little he had accomplished. Sam Darby read his thoughts at once.

"Discouraging, isn't it?" Sam said. "It always is when you start, but as a miner you get used to it. You learn that if you keep at it you'll see results. I'll go next." He took the pickax and, despite his bad leg, climbed to the top of the mound and, somehow bracing himself, he began to swing the tool. He soon had dirt and rock flying in a steady stream. Experience asserting itself again, Fargo thought, and smiled in admiration. When Sam finally halted, Bess took the ax and began to work. She did as well as she could—lacking both strength and experience—and Fargo was grateful. Every little bit helped. When he took his turn again he attacked the top of the mound with new vigor. "Not so hard. Slow and steady. Wear the dirt down, not yourself," Sam called up, and Fargo slowed, let himself fall into a rhythm and felt the difference at once.

Sam took his turn next, then Bess, the cycle in place, and they worked for the most part wordlessly. The hours faded into each other and Fargo stayed the longest atop the mound. They were making some progress but not nearly enough, he saw, glancing down at the pile of dirt they'd cleared away. He had no idea how many hours had passed and he was halfway through his shift when he felt the shallowness of his breath. He halted and slid down to the bottom and met Sam Darby's eyes. "Short strokes and short breaths from now on," the man said as he climbed onto the mound. When it was his turn again he took Sam's advice as he began to work.

The beginnings of a crawl space had been carved out, he saw, enough for him to fit his body in between the top of the earth-and-rock mound and the tunnel roof. But he had to swing the pickax in an awkward, horizontal motion, sometimes lying on his back. When he finally slid down to face Sam his lips were a grim line. "No good. It'll take too long. It's too cramped for the pickax," he said.

"I'll be back," Sam said, and hurried down the mine shaft to return minutes later with two truncated shovels, most of the handles broken off each. "We'll use these as spades. We use the pickax only if we hit hard rock," Sam said, took one with him, and left the other with Fargo. "It's better," Sam called down. "You can get your shoulders into it." When it was his turn again, Fargo felt a surge of encouragement sweep through him as the spade-shovels let him dig out deeper chunks of dirt and sweep them aside. They had to use the pickax only a half-dozen times as the hours rolled on. Soon Fargo could fit his entire body into the crawl space that had been carved out.

But when he came down to rest he slumped against the shaft wall and felt the heaviness in the air. Sam lasted only a short while before he came down and Bess even less. Fargo met Sam's eyes as he began to climb up to attack the earthen mound again and there was no need for words. They were running out of air. He lay on his stomach in the space they had eked out of the earthen wall, dug with the shovel-spade, rested, dug again, cursed silently. The tiredness was more of a creeping lethargy brought on by the decrease of oxygen. He stayed at it a while longer, then slid down, then Sam pulled himself up to work as long as he could before sliding back down.

Bess rose to take her turn, swayed, and Fargo put his arms around her and lowered her to the ground. "Always wondered what it'd be like being buried alive," Sam muttered. "Heard about it happening often enough. I'm sorry I ever wondered now." Fargo swore and climbed to the crawl space again and began to dig with the shovel. But he felt the strength leaving his arms, his entire body, and he cursed with frustrated anger as he dug at the earth wall. He rested, realized his arms were trembling and he was gasping in air, but there was nothing filling his lungs.

He knew they had to have worked through the night but there was no way of knowing how much of the earth wall still remained in front of them. Sam's guess of how long the air would last was proving itself deadly accurate. Fargo attacked the dirt and rock again, drawing on his last bit of strength, hearing the harsh sound of his own breathing as he dug frantically. Finally, he collapsed face down in the crawl space they had managed to carve out. It was a real effort to draw a breath now and each time he did he felt the burning inside his lungs. He felt his eyes close and cursed as he snapped them open. But that final sleep pulled at him again. He hadn't even the strength, nor the will, to slide back down to Sam and Bess. He felt the pickax against his leg, closed one hand around it and drew it forward, almost as a child draws a favorite toy to it.

His eyes were closing again and once more he forced them open. He was faintly surprised there was no coughing, no rasping for breath, only the lulling lethargy that would have no end. With a last burst of rage, he held the pickax in front of him, one pointed end out, managed to rise to his knees, and drove himself forward. He heard his last shout of desperate, frustrated anger as, putting his entire body behind the pickax, he plunged it into the wall of earth.

He felt the wall shudder, then fall away as the pickax plunged through it. The wave of air struck at his face through the narrow opening, hardly a deluge, yet more than enough. It flowed into his opened mouth, around him, rushing past his prone body and down the crawl space. Fargo heard himself half-laughing, half-crying out and he lay still, let the air continue to rush past him until, his lungs finally filled, he pushed his way backward and slid down to the base of the shaft. Bess and Sam were standing, drawing in gulps of air, and Bess fell into his arms. The relief in Sam's eyes needed no words. "What happened?" the man asked finally.

"Never give up. I almost did," Fargo said. He rested a while longer and then rose to his feet. "Follow me. We can finish breaking through together."

When Fargo crawled to the life-giving gap in the

earthen wall he knocked aside more dirt and saw the mine entrance below. He also saw daylight, and Sam helped him clear away enough dirt to fit himself through to the other side. Fargo paused there and helped pull Bess through; Sam crawled out last. Sliding down to the mine entrance, Fargo saw the sun of morning outside. "You two stay here," he said.

"You think they're still watching the entrance?" Bess asked.

"No, but they could be in the house and they'd sure see us riding away. I don't want that," Fargo said. "Give me a half-hour. If I'm not back, you're on your own. Take the sorrel and try to make it to Sarah."

Bess pressed her mouth to his before he crawled from the mine. He stayed on one knee as he peered down the hillside. The house was hidden from view by the hill in front of him and, moving in a crouch, he began to dart forward on foot, leaving the Ovaro with the sorrel. He darted from one cluster of shadbush to another as he made his way down the hillside, pausing beneath a scraggly hawthorn as he came in sight of the house. He saw no one in the yard and ran to where another knot of shadbush grew along the hillside.

He was nearing the house, staying at a crouch as he moved from cover to cover, when suddenly he saw the door open. Roger came out, tossed a bucket of water on the ground, and returned to the house. Fargo, moving on swift, silent feet, raced down and to the rear of the house where he halted and peered in through one of the windows. He saw Roger tying a cardboard box, three traveling bags in the center of the floor. He waited but Linda didn't appear, and he drew his Colt, then silently pushed the window up and swung himself into the house. Roger had finished tying the box when Fargo stepped into the room.

"Going away?" Fargo inquired mildly, and Roger spun, his jaw dropping open. Roger's lips moved but no sound came from them. "Look on me as your friendly neighborhood ghost," Fargo said. "Drop your gunbelt."

Roger exploded in desperation, panic, and his normal nervous instability. He grabbed for his gun and had it only halfway out of the holster when Fargo's shot shattered his kneecap. Roger fell to the floor screaming in pain and clutching his knee as Fargo stepped to him and took his gun. "Oh, Jesus, oh, God. I need a doctor," Roger cried out.

"In time," Fargo said. "Where's Linda?"

"Gone to town to get a wagon," Roger groaned. "Get me to a doctor."

"When will she be back?" Fargo asked.

"Soon," Roger said as he rolled on the floor. Fargo went to him, took him by the back of his shirt, and dragged him into a bedroom. He ripped a curtain to tie up Roger, who continued to groan and moan in pain. Shoving a piece of the curtain into Roger's mouth, Fargo tied the gag on tight and closed the door to the room as he left. Back in the living room, he sat down facing the door to wait, the Colt in his hand. He let some fifteen minutes go by and still Linda hadn't returned. Frowning, he moved to peer out the window to the front of the house and saw no one. Perhaps Roger's definition of soon was a loose one, he reasoned and he moved back to the center of the room and away from the windows.

He didn't sit down this time but stayed on his feet as he faced the door, his ears listening for the sound of a wagon rolling to a halt. But there was only silence and another fifteen minutes went by. The furrow on his brow had become a frown when he felt himself grow cold. "Don't turn around, Fargo," a voice said. He obeyed, stayed motionless, and felt the Colt pulled from his hand. He turned then to see Linda, an old Remington .44 in her hand, his Colt pushed into the belt she wore over a black skirt and black shirt. "I never underestimate anyone twice," Linda said.

"Seems not," Fargo said.

"I never thought you'd leave that old mine shaft alive," she said. "Still, you'd impressed me. I decided to take no chances. When I went to town I left orders with Roger to leave a flowerpot a quarter-mile down the road if everything was all right. It wasn't there."

"You know Roger's unreliable," Fargo remarked.

"Not that unreliable. I left the wagon and came around the back on foot," she said. "Where is Roger?"

"Resting in his room. He has a sore knee," Fargo said.

"Bastard," Linda said, more of a comment than a curse.

"I could've killed him," Fargo said.

"Why didn't you?"

"He's not worth killing. Besides, it'll hurt him more to spend the rest of his life in a cell thinking about what almost was," Fargo said.

Linda's smile was sudden and almost wry. "Am I worth killing?" she asked.

"Yes," he said. "A shame but true." His eyes measured the distance to the Remington she held and he cursed silently. He needed something to give him an added split second, a few paces closer, or something to take her attention from him for an instant. He tried to move toward her.

"Another step and you're dead, Fargo," Linda said.

He shrugged. "Seems that's what I'm going to be anyway," he said.

"You want to hurry it up? Be my guest," Linda said, and he stayed in place. She smiled again. "Didn't think so. Never saw anyone who wanted to speed up their own funeral. But you won't have a long wait. Roger and I have to be on our way."

"What if I said I wanted to go with you?" Fargo asked, stalling for time. "I could keep my mouth shut and it would be fun. You know that. Your memory can't fade that fast."

He saw Linda's tongue slide across her lips. "No, not that fast. But I'll make it fade," she said. He searched for something else to say when the moment he needed suddenly came. He saw Linda's eyes flick past him, the furrow touch her brow, as she glanced through the window. He half-turned, saw Bess and Sam riding down the hillside on the sorrel. He seized the instant, half-dropped, and dived in a flying tackle. Linda's shot scraped the top of his head as he barreled into her. She went down on her back, tried to bring the pistol around to fire again, but he knocked it from her hand with a backhanded blow.

He sat straddling her as he retrieved his Colt and smiled down at her. "Anything seem familiar to you, honey?" he asked.

"Bastard," Linda hissed, and her hands came up, nails reaching for his eyes. He managed to get his arms up in time, brought a quick, short chopping blow down onto her chin, and she went limp.

"Different climax this time," he muttered and rose, let her come to, and yanked her to her feet. He used the rope Roger had tied the box with and bound Linda hand and foot, then tied her into a straight-backed chair. Then he took the cord from the window curtains and tied the chair to the heavy breakfront at one side of the room. Her cool-blue eyes shot fury at him. "Wouldn't want you going anywhere," he said as he strode from the room. He left the house, climbed the hillside to where the Ovaro still waited outside the mine, and raced the horse after Sam and Bess. He caught them as they started up High Cliff Road.

"Oh, God, you're safe," Bess said.

"You know the sheriff in town, Sam?" Fargo asked.

"Yes, Will Henke. Good man," Sam said.

"Let's go. We've a lot to tell him, especially you, Sam," Fargo said.

9

Fargo sat quietly astride the Ovaro alongside the road and let his thoughts unreel as he waited. The sheriff had listened to everything and gone back to the house with them to put Linda and Roger into irons. Fargo had convinced the sheriff to let him finish the last thing that needed to be done. The stage depot master told him that Albert Darnville had taken the stage for Sioux City. Fargo had ridden hard through most of the night, resting only occasionally, taking short-cuts that had finally brought him to the road southeast that ran all the way into Sioux City.

He moved the Ovaro forward as the stage finally came into sight and saw the driver rein up as Fargo blocked his path. The driver had a guard alongside him and the man raised a rifle. "No trouble, friends," Fargo said as he brought the Ovaro alongside the coach and peered in. Albert Darnville was the only passenger.

The man stuck his head out of the window of the coach. "Still turning up at unexpected times and places, Fargo?" Darnville smiled.

"I quit working for Linda Ayler," Fargo said.

"Probably a good choice," Darnville said. "She's a hard woman and I supsect, rather unscrupulous."

"You don't know the half of it," Fargo said. "Mind stepping outside?"

Darnville shrugged and clambered from the coach. Fargo dismounted and ran his hands over the man. "I don't carry guns, not usually," Darnville said. Fargo saw the driver and the guard looking on, confusion and uncertainty in their faces, but the guard had lowered the rifle.

"Got some bad news for you," Fargo said. "You paid a lot of money for a gold mine that's not worth shit." He enjoyed the frown that came to Darnville's face.

"You're crazy. I had my assayer test the gold," Darnville said.

"It's a long story. I'll only give you the highlights," Fargo said and quickly told Darnville how the Aylers had swindled him. Darnville stared into space, his face ashen, when Fargo finished.

"My God," the man breathed.

"They're in jail," Fargo said, and Darnville's face brightened.

"Then I can get my money back," he said.

"Not exactly," Fargo said. "You're joining them."

"Nonsense. I'm a victim. You can't put a man in jail for being swindled," Darnville said.

"No, but you can put him in jail for murder. You had Chet Beamer killed," Fargo said.

"That note? It's torn up already and nobody's going to believe Linda Ayler now," Darnville said.

"No, but they'll believe me. I heard you admit it, remember?" Fargo said. Darnville stared at him, then suddenly whirled to the two men atop the stage.

"Shoot him," he screamed. The guard, still uncertain, started to bring his rifle up and Fargo's Colt stared into his face.

"Drop the gun. I've no quarrel with you boys," Fargo said. The guard dropped the rifle and Fargo turned to see Darnville swing at him. Fargo ducked away from the blow and Darnville stumbled forward. Fargo brought the butt of the Colt down on Darnville's head and the man fall face down and lay still. "You boys have some lariat?" Fargo asked the driver.

"Yes, sir," the man said.

"Tie him up good and we'll go back to Black Hills Junction. You might get a bonus for this trip," Fargo said.

He led the way back when the stage was turned and reached the sheriff's office just before dark. Will Henke greeted him. "Adjoining cells?" the sheriff grinned.

"I'd like that," Fargo said, and watched as Darnville was locked into the cell next to Linda and Roger, only the bars separating them. He left them screaming curses at each other, climbed onto the Ovaro, and rode to the hotel. Bess was there waiting for him as she'd promised.

"You'll have to stay around for the trial," Bess said as she slid into bed beside him.

"Guess so," he said.

"I'll leave you just enough strength to testify," she said. He smiled. It was the kind of sentence he liked.

LOOKING FORWARD!
The following is the opening
section from the next novel in the exciting
Trailsman series from Signet:
THE TRAILSMAN #143
DEATHBLOW TRAIL

*1860, New Mexico Territory, now the state
of Arizona. The Butterfield Overland Trail,
the most dreaded and dangerous track
in the West, where a secret revenge turned
this living hell into a diabolical deathtrap.*

The pinto began to go short just after crossing Dead Man's Wash. Skye Fargo felt it immediately—the subtle shift in the horse's stride. The alteration in the gait was so slight that another man might not have noticed. But Fargo knew it spelled trouble.

After thousands of miles on the trail, Fargo knew every rhythm and movement of his black-and-white mount. He knew its canter and its four-beat fast gallop. He knew the way it took a scramble up a clay bank or a surefooted plunge down a slippery slope of scree. He knew how far it could run and how long it could travel without water. He'd never seen another horse with the strength of his Ovaro, which kept going long after other men's horses fell to the ground. And now, the pinto was going short.

At the top of the crumbling cliff, Fargo dismounted. He glanced back across the shimmering alkali flats. The deeply etched, dry land rippled under the sun's unrelenting glare. In the oily waves of heat, dark figures appeared and disappeared like distant ghosts. He watched as they danced and wavered on the white-hot flats. There was no one there, Fargo knew. It was only the heat.

Fargo wiped his forehead on his sleeve and bent down to examine the Ovaro's front right. The day before, he had extracted a long thorn from his hoof. He wasn't sure he had gotten it all out. Now he feared the tip of the thorn was still embedded in the center of the pinto's tender hoof.

Sure enough, underneath, just to the inside of the horny laminae, was the angry redness of infection and a slight oozing. Fargo winced. The pinto snorted.

"Easy," he said, letting down the hoof and stroking the Ovaro's neck.

There was nothing he could do. Cutting into the sensitive frog might make the infection worse. It would have to work itself out. But meanwhile, riding the pinto would make the infection worsen. Then it would founder and go lame. The Ovaro needed rest. A week of rest. He'd been riding it hard. And now this.

Fargo wiped his face again and felt sweat trickle down his back. It had been a long trip up from Mexico, heading north. The border was only fifty miles behind him. Just ahead was the Butterfield Overland Trail, which ran east to west. There were towns and way stations along this mail route. His best bet was to swing onto the trail until he hit a settlement, then hole up for a while.

He remembered he was short of cash. He had figured on making a straight run up to Santa Fe and picking up some work immediately. For a moment he wished he hadn't been so generous to the poor ranchers he'd met down in Old Mexico. He could use the money he gave them if he had to stop for a week. But then he thought of their gratitude.

"It was worth it," Fargo said to the pinto, patting its muzzle. "Something will turn up. It always does." But it might be hard to find trailblazing work without the use of his horse.

Fargo pulled the canteen out of his saddlebag and took a swig of the lukewarm water. He poured some into his hat and held it out for the pinto. Afterward, he settled the cool moist hat back on his head and took up the reins in his hand. Riding the pinto would only make the hoof worsen. He set off, leading the Ovaro due north. His boots crunched on the hard dry crust of the alkali desert.

In a few miles, they'd come across the Butterfield Overland Trail. And once they turned onto the trail, they'd eventually get to somewhere.

Jackpot was a motley collection of shelters. At the edge of town stood a saloon with a sign that said CHESTER'S FOLLY—SALOON AND ROOMS. The two-story brick building sported an elaborate cupola and carved tin roofline. A brick building in the middle of nowhere was more than folly, Fargo thought, thinking of hauling tons of brick across the desert. Next to Chester's Folly stood a disintegrating adobe hut and a couple of abandoned shacks which threatened to topple at any moment. Further down the main street was a spanking new general store of yellow lumber and a row of solid adobe offices.

Then Fargo saw what he was looking for—a sturdy corral and stables. The sign read HACKS. BOARD. TRADE. MULES. Underneath the sign, on a shady porch, a man sat balancing on the two back legs of a rickety chair. His hat was pulled down over his face, his bare feet hooked over the railing. A pair of worn boots stood beside his chair.

Fargo was just beginning to wonder why a town would spring up here when he spotted the well. It was dug in the center of the main street and had a weathered board collar. Beside it, a rusty pump perched on the edge of the watering trough like a thirsty vulture. After he watered the pinto, he led it toward the stable.

"How do?" The man said, pushing up his hat. His face was deep-lined with living and his eyes squinted shut in the sun.

"How much to put up my pinto for a week?" Fargo asked. "Best feed. Good curry every day?"

The man squinted his eyes almost shut as he turned his face toward the Ovaro. He pulled on his boots.

"Nice pony," he said at last. "Best I've seen in a long time." He walked over and reached out a hand to stroke the pinto's flank gently. "Be a pleasure to board it. Make it five dollars for the week."

Fargo nodded. Not as bad as he feared. Some of these towns had inflated prices for everything, since they had you over a barrel. He'd have enough money for meals. But it would be tight. He'd have to sleep out in the open. He shrugged. He didn't like hotels anyway, folly or not.

"Fine," he said. "Here's half in advance. I'll be in town and I'll look in. Is there any work around here? Maybe for a week or so."

"Work?" the stable man asked. "Hell, if you're good with a rope or a horse you can find something easy." The man looked Fargo up and down. "A big man like you can find something right off. Problem with this town is, we got no able-bodied men left."

"Why's that?" Fargo asked.

"Ain't you heard about the gold rushes going on? Why, every man who can tear loose from his ranch has skedaddled on north into Colorado or west into the desert. The damn town's plumb deserted." He took the reins of the pinto and began to lead it into the corral. "A big man like you won't have any trouble picking up something," he called out over his shoulder. "Ask over at Chester's."

"Much obliged," Fargo said. His stomach was rumbling. He'd get a good meal and scout out his prospects.

Just then he heard the pounding of hooves and a stagecoach swung into view, coming on fast. Two men rode on top, the driver, and another man packing a rifle. The coach came to a halt in front of the stable. The two men hopped down and began to untether the team with the help of the stable man. Within moments, the three of them had the team out of harness and were leading them toward the corrals, ready to switch to fresh horses.

The coach was a rugged Concord with iron-shod wheels, built to withstand the pounding of the rocky trail. Its wine-colored cab was coated with dust. The door opened and a tall man jumped down. He was dressed in the glaring white duds of a professional gambling man, his vest crossed by the gleaming gold chain of a watch fob. The gambler glanced down the deserted street of Jackpot, grimaced, and donned his wide-brimmed hat. Then he pulled the step out from underneath the stagecoach and offered his arm to help someone down.

A small foot in a yellow bowed shoe felt tentatively for the step. Then Fargo saw a shapely leg and a swirl of skirt as a woman in a blue striped dress climbed down out of the stagecoach. She was beautiful, Fargo saw. Her dress clung to every willowy curve. Her neck was long and graceful, seeming too frail to support the weight of the gleaming blonde hair piled on top of her head. She nodded to the gambling man and they spoke a word or two. Then they parted.

Other passengers disembarked. Some stretched and others leaned against the dusty wheels. Fargo watched as the gambler headed up the street and stopped to ask someone something. The man pointed to the edge of town. Undoubtedly Chester's Folly, Fargo thought. He watched the gambler disappear into the brick saloon.

The blonde woman wended her way up the main street, taking no notice of Fargo. She looked into the windows of the general store and then read the signs in each of the adobe offices, making her way slowly up the street. A man doffed his hat to her and followed her with his eyes. The woman walking with him gave his arm a resentful tug. The blonde woman didn't seem to notice.

A fresh team of horses was hitched to the stagecoach now and the driver and the guard were climbing back on top while the waiting passengers climbed back inside. The driver cracked his whip and the coach pulled out.

As the dust settled, Fargo sighted trouble. Two men appeared at the other end of the street, leaning on one another and staggering down the mostly deserted street. One held a half-filled liquor bottle. They spotted the woman in her blue striped dress immediately and headed straight for her, making catcalls. Fargo saw her shoulders stiffen as she continued to look into the store windows, pretending not to notice the two approaching drunks.

Fargo hastened forward just as the men reached her.

"Why, a lush . . . lush . . . luscious critter like yourself shouldn't be walking about here unescorted," the unshaven fat one was saying. He held his arm out to her. She pulled her skirts back and tried to push by him and continue up the boardwalk, but the other stepped in front of her and put his hand against the wall to stop her progress.

"I don't think we've met, yet," he said, his dark eyes unfocused. He hiccupped. The woman was starting to panic.

"No, I don't think we have," Fargo said loudly. The two men jumped and whirled about to face him. The fat one raised the bottle and brought it crashing against the wall, then held up the crown of sharp glass in front of him. The other sidled down the stairs. Fargo saw that they were both unarmed. And drunk. It was hardly a fair fight. The first one came barreling toward him and Fargo put out his foot at the last moment. The man sprawled flat into the dust.

The second one, holding the bottle, came at him shouting, and Fargo ducked to one side suddenly, gave him his shoulder, and the men fell forward onto his friend. Fargo leaned over and removed the bottle from the man's grip.

"You two behave with strangers," Fargo admonished. "Doesn't help the town's reputation."

He straightened up and looked about. The blonde woman had vanished. Fargo walked slowly down the block trying to spot her.

Just then, Fargo sighted a familiar figure hurrying up the street. The tall, slender man walked quickly with his head down, seeming to study the ground in front of him. Under one arm, he carried a thick sheaf of papers and a bulky iron strongbox. Fargo stepped into his path and drew his Colt.

"Halt, you goddamn jackass lawyer," Fargo said. "If there's one thing I can't stand it's seeing a lawyer loose on the streets of a law-abiding town."

The man, seeing the gun drawn, stopped dead in his tracks. His eyes traveled slowly up to Fargo's face, his dark bushy eyebrows lowering impatiently, his body tense. Then his face broke into a smile.

"Skye! Skye Fargo!" he said. "What the hell are you doing in this godforsaken town?" Fargo grinned and holstered the pistol, gesturing toward the two drunks struggling to their feet in the middle of the street a block back.

"Keeping some drunks in line. But I might ask you the same question, Mr. Nathan Levin, Esquire. Last time I ran into you, you were trying to get the Ogallala Gang strung up in Kansas City."

"By God, I was," Nathan said, chuckling. "Did it,

too. All seven of them. Damn, those were glory days."

"So what brings you to Jackpot?"

"Land claims," Nathan said. "I came down here a year ago to settle a case. I hadn't planned to stay. But then word got out that I could get land claims settled fast and ..." Nathan held up the sheaf of papers in front of him. "Well, now I got more work than I can possibly handle."

"So it seems," Fargo said.

"And what brings you here?" Nathan asked. "Just passing through?"

"My horse got a bad hoof," Fargo said. "I stabled it and I'll be around about a week. Looking for a quick job. Then I'm heading up to Santa Fe."

"Really?" Nathan bit his lower lip and his eyes took on a faraway look.

"But right now, I'm heading to Chester's for some chow," Fargo said. "Care to join me? I don't usually eat with lawyers, but in your case, I'll make an exception."

Nathan nodded slowly.

"I've got a better idea," he said. "I've got something in this strongbox that's interesting. Really interesting." He held the iron box in front of him and tapped it with one finger. "I'm going to meet with some clients to discuss the contents. Come along and listen. This might be just what you're looking for."

Nathan Levin led the way to one of the adobe office buildings, opened the door, and ushered Fargo inside. They passed through an outer office filled with desks and file cabinets and into another, larger room where several people waited.

Fargo immediately sighted the pretty blonde

woman in the blue striped dress who had arrived on the stagecoach. She sat demurely on the edge of a chair, her gaze fixed on her shoes. She looked up when they entered, her eyes flicked over Nathan Levin and came to rest on Fargo. He smiled at her and her brows raised slightly. Then she glanced down again, as if embarrassed.

Nathan took his place behind a desk at the center of the room and began to arrange the papers into piles. Fargo examined the other people assembled. There were four in addition to the blonde.

Near the desk sat an older man, probably Mexican, his jet-black hair streaked with gray and his face weathered by a life outdoors. His hands were rough, his clothes those of a rancher. Beside him was a young woman, her long dark hair flowing over her shoulders. She wore a colorful cotton shawl and a broad silver necklace that made her skin and round eyes look even darker. She noticed Fargo's gaze and smiled at him.

On one side of the desk stood a preacher, collar and all. His severe black clothes hugged his thin body, which contrasted oddly with the florid fleshy face. He grasped a well-worn Bible under one arm as though afraid to let it go. He glanced suspiciously at Fargo.

On the other side of the room, a tall muscular black man leaned against the wall. He, too, wore the clothes of a rancher, a length of rope looped through his belt. His wiry hair was close-cropped. His forehead was wide and deep-lined, though he appeared to be a young man. He returned Fargo's gaze but his face betrayed absolutely nothing.

It was a strange group, Fargo thought. He was just

wondering what could have possibly brought them together when Nathan finished arranging the papers on the desk and cleared his throat.

"As you know, we're here today for the reading of the last will and testament of Obadiah Hanbury," Nathan said. "I contacted you all to come as quickly as possible for reasons that will soon become clear."

"There had better be a good reason," the preacher growled under his breath. "I went to a lot of trouble getting out here."

"I'm sure," Nathan said quickly. "Let me explain something before we read the will. This document," he tapped the iron strongbox which stood on the desk, "came into my possession two weeks ago. Obadiah Hanbury died of gunshot wounds in Doubtful Canyon over a year ago. He dictated the will to one of the Butterfield Trail agents. The agent thought Hanbury was out of his head and he didn't take the will seriously, so it was stored at the way station nearby and then forgotten. As soon as it was shipped here, I read it and began to track you down. Now, let's get to business."

The young, dark-haired girl shifted excitedly in her chair and smiled at the man next to her. He patted her shoulder. Probably her father, Fargo thought.

Nathan unlocked the iron box and extracted a document from it, opened it, and began to read: "I, Obadiah Hanbury, known by my friends as Hanby, being of sound mind and body, do hereby make my last will and testament. I want to leave everything to five persons important to me. And I'd like to say something to each of them. Firstly, to my only brother and relative, Reverend Abisha Hanbury, I would say please don't blame me for going west. I did what I had to do."

The preacher shifted uncomfortably and stared at Nathan.

"To Xavier and his daughter Martita Alvarez, I send my appreciation for saving my life that time I got shot up down near the border."

The father and daughter exchanged glances.

"And William Moses Hanbury, who took my name when I freed him from the bonds of slavery. I thank Willy for his devotion to me. I could have known no finer man."

The preacher shot a dark look at William Moses, but the expression on the black man's face never changed. Fargo saw a slight twitch along the side of the man's jaw.

"And, finally to Arabella Sullivan, I send my undying affection. She should know that it was for her that I left the comforts of civilization far behind, following the dream of riches, so that one day I could make her happy. That day has come, but I fear I will not be there to enjoy it."

The blonde in the blue striped dress bent her head down further so that no one could see her face. Nathan glanced around the room at each of them in turn. Then he continued reading:

"I, Hanby, am lying here in Doubtful Canyon dictating this will to a Butterfield Trail agent. The banditos shot me up good this time and I don't think I'll recover. For the last three years of my life, I've been prospecting down near the San Pedro River. And last month, I wandered up around the town of Coronado where I finally found what I have been looking for. The mother lode, pure gold. I believe it's the biggest and richest gold deposit ever found in the West. Near as I can tell, the gold line drives straight up the hillside and goes deep. There's enough there for a thousand fortunes.

"And I'm leaving it to these five mentioned in this will. The Coronado mine is theirs to share equally by all those five left living, and to remember me as I have remembered them. Signed this day, the fourteenth of July in the year 1859, Obadiah Hanbury."

Nathan put the document down slowly. There was a long silence in the room. Xavier Alvarez shook his graying head.

"A gold mine," he muttered. "Belonging to me."

"Belonging to us, you mean," Reverend Hanbury cut in.

Fargo glanced at Arabella Sullivan. She sat swinging her feet and looking down at her shoes.

"Why, Hanby," Arabella said, almost to herself. "I never figured you'd make out so well."

William Moses, standing alone against the wall, caught Fargo's eye and shook his head slowly from side to side. Fargo couldn't read his expression. Martita and her father began to chatter in Spanish.

"There's a problem, though," Nathan Levin cut in.

"What kind of problem could there possibly be?" Arabella asked. Her voice was pleasingly soft. "Seems to me the five of us just inherited a gold mine from Hanby."

"God rest his soul," the reverend added.

"That's right," Nathan said. "But Hanby was heading back here to Jackpot to renew his claim on the land. You see, he only had rights to it for one year. That year expires in exactly ten days."

"So?" the reverend said. "Surely you can fix it for

us right here. You're a lawyer. You could renew the claim and we could all sign it.''

"It doesn't work that way out here,'' Nathan said slowly. "You see, you've got to take possession of the claim. In person. Then it can be renewed on paper. That's the law.''

"Fine,'' Arabella said briskly. "We go to this gold mine and take possession. Where is Coronado, anyway?''

"Way the hell down on the San Pedro River,'' Fargo cut in. They all turned to look at him. "It's a hundred miles along the roughest trail in the West, right through the middle of Apache territory, where the Mexican banditos are thicker than flies and there's not enough water to wet a rattlesnake's tongue. And to get to Coronado, you go to the San Pedro River and turn south. It's in the middle of the worst desert in the country.''

"Who is this man?'' the reverend cut in. "What gives him the right to listen to our business? If this gold mine is so valuable, I'm not certain I want everybody in the territory knowing about it.''

"Mr. Skye Fargo is an associate of mine,'' Nathan Levin said. "He's here at my invitation. I'll vouch for him.''

"Skye Fargo?'' Xavier Alvarez repeated, looking over the tall figure, head to toe. "We have heard many stories about Skye Fargo. You are a very famous man. So famous to be called Señor Trailsman. Is that you?''

"Never mind about him,'' the reverend interrupted. "So this gold mine is hard to get to. Okay. Maybe we send Mr. Alvarez here as our representative. He's used to this country.''

"Unfortunately," Nathan said, "your brother was no lawyer. When he dictated his will, he specified that the mine would belong to all those five left living. I'm afraid that means that all five of you have to take possession of the mine. That means all of you have to travel to Coronado."

The Reverend swallowed hard and Arabella's eyes widened.

"There's one more problem," Nathan said. "Hanby's claim expires in exactly ten days. On the first of August. Last week, I had a message from the local authorities in the town of Coronado. Word's gotten out that in ten days this gold mine will be up for grabs. Prospectors have already gathered in Coronado from all over the territory. On the morning of August first, when the sun comes up, either the five of you will be there to stake your claim, or it'll be a gold rush that will make '49 look like a Sunday picnic."

"Can we make it to Coronado in ten days?" the reverend asked.

"In six days, if there's no problem on the trail," Nathan said.

"What if ... what if we go," Arabella said hesitantly, "and ... Indians ... or something happens to one of us on the way?"

"Good question," Nathan said. "According to the will, if one of you dies, then the gold mine is still bequeathed to the survivors. It would just be split four ways instead of five."

Arabella nodded and looked down again at her shoes.

"What if one of us doesn't want to come? What if one of us doesn't care about any gold mine?" William, the black man, asked in his deep booming voice. It was the first time he had spoken and everyone turned to look at him.

"Well, then the other four couldn't take possession," Nathan answered. "Is there anybody here who doesn't want to go?"

Fargo saw Willy's jaw tighten again. He shifted his weight from one foot to the other and continued to lean against the wall.

"So," the reverend said, "you're telling us we have only one choice. We have ten days to go across this Butter . . . butter . . ."

"Butterfield Overland Trail," Fargo put in.

". . . Is that what you're telling us?"

"That's about it," Nathan said.

"Well," Arabella put in, "we'll just take the stagecoach. I came to Jackpot on the stage."

"There won't be another stagecoach for a week," Nathan said.

"A week will be too late," said Alvarez. "We could hire mules. Or horses."

"I can't ride all the way on a horse. And neither can this lady," the Reverend said, gesturing to Arabella and pointedly ignoring Martita Alvarez. "Are you sure there isn't a stagecoach of some kind around here?"

"There's an old one at the stables that might be for sale," Nathan said. "But you're going to need someone to guide you. That's rough country out there."

"That is why you brought Mr. Skye Fargo in here, isn't it?" Alvarez asked, grinning at Nathan. Nathan shrugged. "He is the famous Trailsman, who can—"

"But ... but we don't even know this man!" the reverend sputtered. "He could be anybody—"

"Why don't we take a vote?" William's deep voice cut in. "All in favor of hiring Mr. Fargo raise his hand."

William raised his, as did Xavier and Martita. Arabella turned to look at Skye. Her eyes narrowed as if measuring him as she considered whether to raise her hand.

"I don't know this Mr. Fargo well enough to trust him," she said quietly, turning to Nathan.

"We already got the majority," William said. Slowly, Arabella put her hand in the air. The reverend crossed his arms defiantly.

"I guess you're out-voted, Reverend," Nathan said.

"It's a helluva trip," Fargo said. "What's the fee?"

"How about part of a gold mine?" Alvarez asked, his eyes shining.

"Hold on there!" the reverend said. "That's my gold mine you're talking about giving away!"

"Sorry," Fargo answered. "I take my money up front. Two thousand. Take it or leave it."

"That's outrageous!" the reverend protested.

"It's worth it if he gets us there," Arabella said. "It's four hundred each. Let's ante up and get going."

Fargo saw the tall black man start. As the other four approached the table to lay their money down, William jammed his hands down in his pockets, which caught Nathan's attention. Nathan rose and sauntered over and conferred with the man for a moment.

"I'll be staking Mr. Hanbury's part," Nathan said, coming back to the desk and pulling some money out of his pocket to throw down on the table. Fargo rose and approached the pile of money. He took it up and counted it, peeled off three bills, and handed the rest to Nathan.

"Hold on to that until I get back to Jackpot," he said. "I'll go make the arrangements to hire the coach and horses and get supplies. Nathan, I'll meet you at Chester's in a half-hour."

Fargo turned around to address the five Hanby's five survivors.

"You can pay me back later for the supplies. Now, it's a hard trail out there," he said. "Maybe we'll have it easy. Maybe we won't. But once we get out there, you do what I say and we'll get through it all right. We leave in two hours."

Fargo left the room and headed toward the stables.